www.pagebacon.com

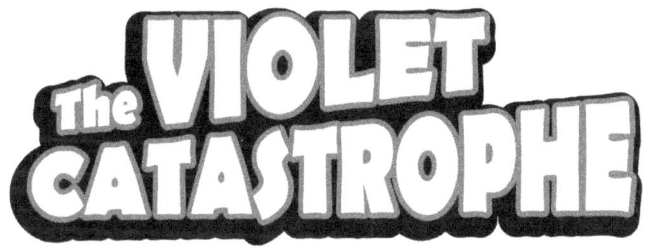

WILL SCHMITZ

ISBN-10: 0-9964147-1-1
ISBN-13: 978-0-9964147-1-5

For Mary

I. IN WHICH THERE IS
SOMETHING TO WAKE UP TO

Wentworth was sleeping on his office's couch, the telephone within arm's length. A series of comets flashed across his eye screen—the effect of having stared too greedily into the strobe light behind a gorgeous Mexican wild woman who had been smuggled over the border.

The detective's claw, paw, hand stretched towards the receiver. The faint image of Packard, Wentworth's partner who had managed to get a Marine to slit his throat in a Tijuana bar fight, flitted across the aching field of Wentworth's brain as a voice on the other end of the hook introduced a job. The pastie that Mr. Luke Wentworth had caught the evening before at the strip show was scratching against something growing in his right trouser pocket.

"Mr. Wentworth?"

"Speaking."

"My name is Jack Poule. I've got a missing daughter. Probably nothing serious. She's taken trips before, shorter ones, without notifying anyone. Can you come to my house for lunch? I'd like to explain the details of the possible case."

"Probable, possible? What's the address?" Wentworth muttered.

Luke began fishing for his socks and his gun as he cradled the receiver in the valley of his bent neck and raised shoulder. The address he was given was in Brentwood. Wentworth's office was near downtown, Olympic and Connecticut.

After a trip to the washroom to admire his stubble and clean himself up, Wentworth was off. He shoved himself behind the wheel of the economy car that he had traded the Charger in for. He sleepily drove through the already boldly active, Erosless megatown.

Poule lived on Foxoro Drive. Wilshire and Sunset were Went's favorite streets. He could have taken the Santa Monica freeway over to the San Diego to get to Poule's place, but Luke preferred boulevarding and looking at the new wild animals that traversed the old trail.

The sweet machines were busy purring the Miracle Mile. There went Orbach's. Wentworth slipped a tape into the deck and on came Handel's Water Music. The LaBrea Tar Pits—it's difficult to escape that feeling of being only gently half-alive. There are palpable dangers to be feared in feeling that way. A petite image of Packard losing his footing and cracking his head against the bar. Luke pulled the pastie from his pocket and tossed it on the dash in order to remember and admire that dancer.

Wentworth pulled up to the electric gate, rolled down his window, pushed the button and announced himself to the inquiring, disembodied female impulses coming over the screened box. Wentworth heard the barking guard dogs. A "Goddamned dogs" light flashed warningly in his cat mind. Luke always considered himself to be a good body-and-fenders man. His biocycle was low this week. This case could turn into a

Golden Gater. He'd push it through.

A valet approached as Luke pulled up before a house the owner was treating like a mansion, but was, in fact, only an enlarged ranchero. The hegemony of this household was likely to be a benevolently oppressive one.

Jack Poule was the most likable man anyone who spends their daily life chasing after dollars could ever meet. He still had his own irregular teeth and kept in good shape by exercising at his club. Poule looked self-confident as he greeted you in his Penguin shirts and light checkered pants. Luke got a quick shake in which he felt there was something ever so slightly missing. "What kept you?" Poule wanted to know.

"I prefer driving Wilshire to the freeway."

Poule could do nothing but smile an amused, "Oh," apologized for asking but added, "lunch had to be kept waiting."

"Sorry. I wasn't told about the time," said Wentworth, passing along the white hallway filled with Courbets and Mezzo-American artifacts on pedestals and shelves.

Poule had to intone a vigorous, "No matter," to remove the look of disappointed reflection in Wentworth's annoyed eyes. "What's your favorite drink, or what would you like to drink?"

"A Lobo will do the trick."

"Fine. I'll have one brought out to you on the terrace. I need to supervise the preparation of some mushrooms, a semi-favorite dish, personally. And so, please excuse me," said Poule, promising his daughter, older daughter, would deliver the drink.

Wentworth walked around the kidney-shaped pool to the raised flower beds planted with annuals. There was a cluster of Pink Dream, Medallion and Maiko mums that particularly distracted Wen's nose and somewhat irritated the pimple opened that morning and from which the pus had been incompletely excised.

The garden was shaded in Devil's Walking-stick and Russian Olive. Wentworth's eyes began to follow a pair of Sleepy Sulpher butterflies as they danced in a kind of tandem parallax pattern along the edge of the bed. Wentworth pushed aside some Verbena to continue watching their flight. He distracted instead by an escadrille of female gymnosophists sunning on a rooftop down below. Three were being nasty. Went was ripped from his five seconds of staring by an amused, almost laughing hand.

Judith Poule was offering him his drink saying, "Interesting, aren't they?" She handed it to him.

Wentworth, caught, summoned grace, and elided the indictment by asking Judith's name.

"Shy, but sly one, aren't you? I'm Judith."

"Will I be leaving today with my head?" Went said to be witty.

"No, but you might not escape getting some," she outdid him and maintained the established tension.

Wentworth was, say, startled and slammed to earth simultaneously. His delicately nervous chuckle capitulated to the lady's superior tongue.

"I didn't know you were adept in the field of hermeneutics, Mr...." Ms. Poule pretended not to know W's business or name.

"Wentworth. Luke Wentworth. What are 'hermeneutics' Miss...." and so it went. The crow baiting the fox with bitter grapes. She was dressed in a purple two piece, was delicious looking and as enticing as a maiden corpse to a necrophiliac.

The luncheon announcement separated the opponents. Each retired reluctantly to their corners.

Luke was fairly angry at being outdone. He swore, "educated cunt," as he fixed a stream into the bathroom bowl. Looking up, there was a seventeenth century travelling Comedia del Arte clown grinning maliciously down at him. Luke hoisted his fly and tried to talk to himself, telling himself he would soon adjust to the climate. He took a look at his eyes. They were still the same color, but dull, either from the drink or being bested by Sheffield-Sharp Lady Judith. Luke didn't appreciate the sensibility that had brought so many ogrish fascinations together under one dumb dome. Luke was against losing face. His pride usually prevented disgrace. Would lunch be gloomy? The Dodgers were supposed to win today. Luke didn't normally find himself out of his own league. But what can be "normal" today? Nothing much, old top. Luke pounded the bathroom wall very lightly, spun around, and went to eat. Why was that such a strong Lobo?

It had been a normal drink. The dining room was lined with African masks. Nine places were already filled, all by women. Four more places were set. Wentworth was overcome with a vermicular foreboding. Judith appeared from a door on the right and escorted Luke to his place. Everyone looked up. The guard dogs were growling nearby. Wentworth grinned. They were a placid lot. Only Ms. Poule possessed the propanolol tongue.

The ladies were chosen by origin or type. Poule had all the bases covered: Black, white, Chinese, Japanese, Hispanic, elderly, bosom, homely, professional, purposeful, casual. Poule going around giving everyone strokes. Jack introduced Wentworth to his staff.

Waiters appeared and the red-haired Poule began to conduct the concert of the conversation. The ladies mostly exchanged detailed client information throughout lunch.

Walnut mushrooms, banana-bacon tidbits, a Roquefort spread and Bourbon hors d'oeuvres were the appetizers. An avocado salad was served and there was a choice between Crabmeat Kentucky Chowder and Shrimp Bisque. Poule made a point of recommending the crabmeat chowder to Wentworth, although he had already requested it.

"Oh," said Poule. He returned to grilling the amply endowed woman as to why her deal for the house behind the Hollywood Bowl hadn't been finalized. The maestro tapped his wand and each bird in the compliant assembly sang him her song. The busty one ended in a shrieking flute exchange. The professional-looking bitch tweeted nicely from her perch. The elderly woman groaned out her chain-smoking tale in bass cello tones.

Luke was happy enough, not seated next to Judith. She sat bored-faced at the far end of the table in the horse latitudes. She had changed into a pink dress. Company policy? All the ladies were dressed either in pink or yellow chiffon. The black woman looked spectacular, even gave Luke a wink after he'd been stealing intermittent glances. Poule saw the exchange and turned to his daughter. They exchanged nods.

A Saint Emilion `52 had been brought out. A good year, and Luke was dumping it down greedily.

"God hides the truth in wine," Miss Poule chided as the waiter again returned to refill to Wentworth's glass.

"A skeletally white hearse followed me most of the way over here. Maybe I'm seeing too much truth today."

No rejoinder. Luke shrugged.

"Has Judith been giving you a dose of her Sorbonne education? Please excuse her if she's been rude," said the fecund Jack. "She feels stifled by what my business has to offer her." Judith's eyes lit briefly with bemused hatred.

Luke had to leave the table just before the main courses of Deviled Lobster Tail Inferno and Chicken in Orange-Lemon Sauce were being brought out. Someone followed until he reached the bathroom door.

Under the hysterically grinning face of the Comedia pastel, the first prophecy was fulfilled. Luke tried to ask questions, but none were answered. "Not now," she said thrusting a business card into his hand.

Although privatized, Luke returned to his meal unblushing. The first look he stole at Ms. Poule revealed that she was wise. A voiceless cackle radiated from her slightly parted lips. She lifted her glass three inches from the table to offer Luke a malicious confidant's toast.

When Luke motioned for another glass of wine to compliment the lobster, his lips received an offensive surprise. The label stated Saint Emilion, but it was distinctly an inferior California wine.

Poule had been watching for Wentworth's reaction. He proffered, "It's been an experiment. Someone's been trying to convince me this substitute could pass, price-wise, for the French. May I offer you six bottles to make amends?" All was forgiven. Poule returned to his and mushrooms on toast.

For dessert, a slice of Bourbon Watermelon. Wentworth tried it for graciousness sake. The chocolate walnut pie that followed erased his hurts. Wentworth was about to light a commercial cigarette when Poule shouted, "Stop! It would be a sin to drown so much splendid flavor with one of those filthy things." He had the servant bring Luke one of his own brand, Turkish. Poule failed to warn Went that the tip of the cigarette he was smoking contained a pellet of hashish.

Soon Wentworth was ready to un-conduct business. His hand strayed under the table where it was met and guided by a friendly manus to a knoll with a spectacular slide down it. A few seconds later, Poule, looking in Luke's direction, dismissed his drones. He invited Wentworth into the study to discuss his wayward daughter. A sad face glanced at him. Before he could get up, Luke had received a second calling card. This was beginning to form an interesting pattern. Luke wondered how much Poule made a day.

Wentworth felt melted in sauce, ready to be served to a hungry giant. As he floated after Poule, Wentworth heard all the courses of the meal start to talk. Being zipped apart by acids and dismembered into acids, proteins and fats. No, let's be a dish that was forgotten in the kitchen, overlooked in the corner of the table, dropped on the floor. "No. You're the monster's favorite dish along with mushrooms and spinach jelly."

Wentworth stumbled, an ungainly pup, behind Poule into his large study-library lined with law books and quadrant maps of the greater Los Angeles area.

"Interested in a house?" Poule asked, pulling Luke out of his clearing fuzziness. Wentworth apologized. Poule smiled and understood. "The devil's mischief is slightly in your way today, Mr. Wentworth. Here's a photograph of my daughter, Alica, and a list of the people I know of who she's been seeing lately."

"How long has she been gone?"

"About three weeks."

"Why wait till now before you start trying to find her?"

"She usually calls after a week or two. I don't hold on tight."

"Have you called in the police?"

"They're looking, but I can afford you. And you come recommended."

"Can I take the photograph?"

"Surely."

"What was your daughter doing before she disappeared?"

"Well, she used to be interested in the arts. Dance and film mainly. Lately, to my astonishment, she's developed an interest in math and science. Three names on that list are of fuddy-duddy professors she dated recently."

"They teach on different campuses."

"Alica goes where she will. She's enrolled in four schools

right now."

There was a knock and the butler entered. Poule was wanted on the phone. Poule excused himself. Wentworth seated himself in a thickly cushioned armchair to scrutinize the photo and contemplate the list.

Two professors' names stuck out. One was a physicist and the other a microbiologist. The third was an economist. None in the natural sciences. There were painters, film-makers (third-rate fascist ones), a (pop-top) regional poet, and a sculptor (fortunately, Luke had no opinion on those). All but the film-makers would be easy to reach. The others were attached to universities and were chained to regular hours. One of the film-makers was shooting a movie in Africa where he'd end up with parasites in his blood. Luke crossed him off the sheet.

Wentworth and the photograph. She had a pair of eyes that flashed the brightness you get when walking through a shaded door into sunlight. She had on a dress that proved she had at least as much humor as her sister. It was patterned with fat clusters off-brown and gray snakes entangled with no beginning or end.

Poule returned, took station behind the massive oak desk. Wentworth looked up from the photo and saw why Poule's greeting had felt different. Two of the tops of Poule's fingers were missing below the nail. Wentworth saw them now, inching caterpillar-like across the black branch of a pen.

"That was the police. They've traced the sculptor. He left for Rome with a female companion on the same day that Alica disappeared. It wasn't her. He had a stroke and is in an Italian hospital. The woman's returned to Chicago. You can scratch him."

Luke dutifully drew a thin line through sculptor. He wondered what a foreign hospital might be like. "Does he speak

Italian?"

"Who?"

"The sculptor."

"Damn it. Why would I want to know?"

"What does Alica speak?"

"French, Italian, German, and Spanish. I hope you're not thinking she's left L.A."

"Why not?"

"She's too involved to have left."

"Involved in what?"

"My business, for one thing. She was closing some important deals for me. I need her back by the end of this week. Now, do you think you can find her?"

"Let me get going then."

"All right. Sorry to be gruff. I'm tense. Worried about her."

"Yes. Well, thank you for the lunch."

"I've had Jeffers put the wine in your car. Call. Leave a message if I'm not in."

"Every day."

"Two hundred dollars a day till Friday, then your usual fee."

"OK. Don't get excited. I'll do my job."

"Goodbye."

Luke knew when he wasn't supposed to say any more. He folded the list, turned round and went to find the door. The sugar coating hadn't taken long to dissolve. He was already wishing that the case had been tossed elsewhere. Angry, Wentworth got the wrong door and stepped out into the west garden, almost onto a pair of naked, newly hatched, yellow beaked sparrows fallen from their nest onto the concrete patio. A beard of ants was moving over their bodies. Wentworth heard a growling from around the edge of the house accompanied by several sets of frantically scampering feet. He zipped back through the sliding doors. The dogs overshot the corner and shot into the center of the yard, stopped, and snapped their jaws at the air. He stared at the dogs a moment, until he became aware of Judith Poule. She was reflected into the opposite middle distance of the grass by the glass over his right shoulder.

"Having thoughts of suicide?"

"Wanna go play somewhere?"

"I'll show you to your car."

"Sure you don't want to?"

"Haven't you had enough for an afternoon?"

"No. Do you want Alica back for love and money too?"

This last question finally hit a nerve. Ms. Poule quieted and allowed Luke to follow silently behind her to the front door. Luke's teeth were tingling. Dogs aroused fear in him. He had been bitten by a farm dog at age three. He had no recollection of the event and couldn't name what generated his phobia.

The house had been cool. It was hot out. Drive back to the office on the surface streets? Best to head for the freeway and forget the sights. To the hunt, Wentworth! Toast the hunt. Your fee is up and the people to be foxed for answers are interesting for a change. Once again—*employed*. He recalled with amusement the rotation of Ms. Poule's rear. It made him smirk awesomely, until he looked back at the hounds trailing his exit from the estate. And away were blasted those smart pleasures.

II. SETTING THE WHEELS IN MOTION AND A PURPOSELESS DREAM

We are the slaves of shadow. Cryptogamous, our every peculiarity. We imagine ourselves to be selecting. But the forms we are embedded in are mocked by the long forgotten taste of the ideas that engendered them. What is *so*?

Wentworth chose his part-time secretary because she was fat, ugly, bright and no temptation. He gave Shirley the list and asked her to arrange interviews as soon as possible.

Luke, no longer trustful of Poule, opened a few bottles of the wine. Two bottles contained the fake stuff. He offered it to Shirley, but wine was something she was also on to, and down the toilet it ran. He gave her a bottle of the real McCoy upon demand. Luke slapped himself on the forehead. The nocuous fluid would have been perfectly acceptable, proudly served, in the home of his ex-wife, Ingrid. Too late. Oh, well.

Wentworth poured himself some scotch and soon fell asleep at his desk. Since reading the Castanets books, Luke sometimes had dreams of flying, but instead of flying through and over earthly landscapes, or merely breaking gravity, Wentworth flew through deep space. He liked to sit in Cassiopeia's chair and invite foreigners for cocktails and delicate discussions about the theories of Boehme, Boileau Despreaux, and Bohr. These socials would often break up once the argument began, as it always did, over whether objective theory would ever geminate beyond its general-purpose paralysis. Blue aliens would begin shouting their strongly gelded, but still ripping obscenities at the obstreperous Gonococcus people. The troubles would erupt. What golems they all were to their precious systems! Wentworth was tired of them. Dung beetles whose Puritan need was to put someone on intellectual dunking stools. W.W. refused to attend any more Puseyite parties.

The atmosphere of the greater part of the office was dusky. Transparent and compact in the mass, but liquid and sparkling at the rifts where a golden clasp of sunlight banded it. Wentworth had the most unusual, in detail, dream of his life. The delineations of surface and plane, space and inhabited area, fused with the idea of his own individual body, seated in a chair, and disappeared. He had broken through the outer membrane of some very thick-skinned conceptions. He now wandered in a zone of discordant equality where every impression received became a disembodied voice trying to whisper a secret about its own existence in an effort to explicate what about itself was most often misperceived. "Mind." Was it any more than a moss cracking through rock with the perverted force of obstinance? Pardon me, but it possesses qualities that would become ne plus ultric if properly massaged.

Outside of his upper room filled with subaqueous light, snakes slid along jungle floors. Manta rays were fornicating under the crowd of waves. The day, full of radiance, was promising a release from thought, death, multitudinous generation and unabating pain. Wentworth was in Japan witnessing, from a telescopic distance, the concerns of two very other lives.

Wentworth was surprised that he understood Japanese so perfectly—could read the characters. Thousands of people were packing themselves into a baseball stadium. It seemed to be the final game of a series. The tickets were all sold out, but scalpers moved through the crowd shouting seat locations and ticket prices. One scalper moved less aggressively to snare prey. He was dressed more like an office clerk than a hustling barker who had been looking forward to tearing viciously into some executive money. His tickets were in excellent locations, yet were offered far below prices being squeezed by the other dozen or so scalpers.

A man in a mouse-gray suit wearing a dark green tie came up to the scalper, showed him a police badge and confiscated the tickets. The gaggle that had gathered to purchase them became furious. What was he doing to this savior? The policeman shouted to them that the tickets were counterfeits.

The seats they supposedly represented were already filled. The crowd began to tear at the poor clerk whose eyes shut. He was clearly more ashamed than miserable and furious at being caught. The policeman intuited his prisoner's strange condition. He dispersed the crowd by promises of justice and threats of prosecution. He placed his prisoner in handcuffs and led him away.

"What is going to happen to me?"

"I have to take you back to Tokyo."

"But I can't leave Kyoto now," he said in despair. "Why aren't you taking me to the local authorities?"

"You've committed forgery of a special nature. It has to be

handled through the central law courts in Tokyo. We leave by the next train."

The sad little clerk was put in the back seat of a detective car. The officer sat in the front talking to the driver about who they thought would win today's game, who their favorite players were, and how long they had been following their teams. Occasionally, the detective would sneak a glance at his captive only to see him staring in aimless melancholy out the rear window at whatever or whomever was passing by. The driver and he joked about the prisoner's difference from other catches.

"This one doesn't have the clever look of any of the others."

"No, this may have been the first time at it. Probably an independent who hasn't had any guides."

"How good are the tickets?"

"Why, no good at all."

"I mean how well are they reproduced? May I look at one?"

The detective handed the driver a ticket that was for a private box. "No smudges. Good job at imitating the color. They'd easily pass for real. How do you tell how they're phony?"

"The serial numbers are wrong."

This conversation took the trio to the station. The two policemen exchanged cordial farewells and promises to have a drink together the next time the detective came to town. They both liked the same players and same teams.

The detective was usually very gruff and curt to the felons he apprehended. They were professionals and so was he. This time he spoke almost softly to his prisoner.

"What direction do you prefer facing when riding on the train?"

"It doesn't matter to me."

The detective explained that he always preferred to sit facing forward, that facing the disappearing rather than the oncoming vistas made him feel uncomfortable and sometimes even ill.

The detective removed the handcuffs. The conductors knew the clerk was a prisoner and there was no place to escape to on the train. Besides, it was almost empty of other passengers.

The detective proposed lunch. He was furiously hungry, on an expense account, and happened to know that the train had an excellent dining car. The clerk still looked pained, but agreed to eat with his captor just the same. It struck them both as funny, in very different ways, to see themselves eating together in a first-class dining car. They were supposed to be aggressive enemies. The more the detective surveyed his captive's demeanor, the more curious he became about him. The prisoner sensed a quiet round of questions coming. This relaxed him tremendously. He desperately wanted to tell his story, even if to this cop.

It was six o'clock. Wentworth was stirred by the sound of a flushing toilet, but he at once returned to the slumberous ceremony that was offering him such an exotic repast. The second sleep, seemed to him, longer than the first and brought with it the present of a feeling of comfort and forgetfulness. It so conclusively abnegated the desire to wake that he would have almost been happy to die. All his narcotic longings ceased. The madreporic community that made up so many marred facets of his existence became insignificant. The normal anxiety to "live" was almost effaced. Red Admirals fluttered through his toes. The invisible presence of numberless birds (taking up one another's song) was close beside him when Luke again felt eased into dream.

They had dinner; sashimi, tempura, battered vegetables, plenty of saké. And through it, the two men began to like one another. It's never hard to become envious of another person's life. They smoked cigarettes through the drinking. The detective wanted out of his job. He had assumed that was what his prisoner had been trying to do by selling phony tickets to a frenzied baseball throng. To get out of one's life, one's old skin, and be able to appear fresh without worrying about how long the new life would last in this world obeisant to paper commandments.

That was not at all it for the prisoner. This surprised the detective. He had noticed that the clerk had bad teeth and mentally cringed thinking of the numerous times the clerk must have to submit to the company dentist's drill. The detective was balding. The clerk preferred having bad teeth (and he didn't go to the company dentist or go all that often to his own) to a bald head. The clerk has assessed the cop as smugly overweight.

He considered himself a product of personal will rather than environment. What did that matter? He was the one caught and the detective knew it.

The mousey-looking clerk's wife had run off shortly after having given birth to the couple's only child, a daughter, Nikko. The detective had a niece with the same name. The train was passing through a small, but heavily industrialized area. The clerk interrupted his confession to ask permission to close the window because of the sulfureous fumes.

"Please do." They bothered the detective too. Polite interest in the story had prevented him from responding with more vigor to the unpleasant smell. The wife had disappeared with the family funds to Europe. She sent postcards from Zurich where she was studying music. They apologized, confessed guilt, said how much she still felt the need to live, and why she could never come back.

The little girl had grown up unable to articulate feminine genders. Everything was "its" or "his." The clerk had tried finding another mother, but since he was legally married and proved stubborn about divorce, he had not been able to find another woman. Besides, his salary remained the size it was when his wife left.

All had gone well, the two of them were happy and he adored watching his daughter smile, develop and grow. "She could light a new heaven," he told the detective. Every bit of money that was not going into their essential living expenses went into buying books, clothes, lessons and gifts for the child.

"Why the counterfeit tickets then, if you are both happy and seem to be able to satisfy your essential needs? It's not college money that you need is it? Even selling tickets you couldn't make enough to get that."

"No," the clerk began to cry, "my daughter's developed myiasis in the poor quarters I've forced us to live in. We would have had enough, but now she's in the hospital. I'm unable to pay the bills."

"But what is 'mi e i sis'?"

"An almost extinct malady in modern times, Sir. It's an infestation of the body by fly maggots. Their eggs must have been in the water that we were drinking."

The detective was shocked and began to cry also. The clerk and he sat at their table and sobbed together, neither able to say a word for they each had reached where heartache does not submit the bastardizations of speech.

The detective's impulse was to—but here Wentworth was rousted Shirley, who was shrilly saying, "Can I go home now?" Luke could have cut her up for goldfish food. If he'd had anything in his hand he would have thrown it. She tried as nicely as she knew how to apologize. It wasn't hard to see that the boss was "disturbed." Shirley hurried on to the business she had accomplished while he had been "away." Dragged back into the slime of his own reality accelerated Wentworth's blood-lust.

Shirley had never seen him quite this bad. Though Barbara,

Went's ex, had, Shirley now remembered, warned her about this kind of mood in the dick. "Rage would be a euphemism for what he's like when he's pulled prematurely out of one of what he considers his personally triumphant euphorias. He doesn't think any of the rest of us ever get to have such juicy dreams," Barbara'd confided over some chummy drinks.

Wentworth pumped down scotch while Shirley reflected upon her possible fate in the next five seconds. He seemed reasonable by the time she began to respond to his blaring, "Well, what is it!!!"

Shirley revealed Wentworth's schedule of appointments for the following day. Some of the people on Poule's list were dead. A painter and an ex-boxer, just recently. The sculptor was in … Wentworth interrupted to say that he knew about the damned sculptor who'd balled his way into the friggin' Italian hospital. The sculptor was in St. Louis where a show of his was opening in a few days. Wentworth wasn't going to be able to see him until Tuesday.

"He's not in a Roman hospital? Who told you that?"

"His secretary. He hasn't been out of the country in the last year."

"Why is Poule lying to me?!"

"How should I…." Shirley began to reply, but Wentworth was distracted, distraught, and waving her off.

"This might be a real case," happily snapped.

"Do you think you can handle it?" Shirley sarcastically replied to no effect. Wentworth was back in good humor, eager to start the chase.

The sky has closed its wings behind Wentworth's back. Slick businessmen are cruising Sunset Strip to see what a piece of freshness has landed on their sidewalk. Mischievous demons cough out of exhaust pipes. Went wanted to go out and look.

Wentworth's dream had poked him annoyingly in the heart. What had it been looking for? Wentworth's past rolled out for him. His present avenues of thought were crowded with questions. Who to love? Was there anyone left? He still wanted wised-up purity. That myth. Who to believe. Who was the one who wouldn't betray him or measure his deeds with a micrometer? Packard. He's dead. Pack coddled, but never slandered. Vices were acceptable to him. He didn't bore. Who was left? You? No one more amiable exists.

Wentworth wiped away what was almost a tear. He searched with his blind hand for that bottle while he stared out the window at the unambient lights of the shops, street lamps and headlights of the passing vehicles. He should find another partner. Maybe someone young. Wentworth pulled hits from the bottle and thought about himself, Alica, and Mexican whores until the phone rang.

It seemed to be a wrong number. It was a wrong, right number. Wentworth slammed the receiver down. That feeling had been on him. Every feeling free, none denied or strangled. Not often that we get there, or get to stay long.

On came the pouting. Poule, his daughter, and diving agents formed a poussette that pranced 'round him, laughing and sharing secrets. They looked at one another, then sneered at Wentworth. The outcast, never privy to the inner secrets of deals or lusts.

"Too early to get crazy."

Wentworth's routine was to shake down the people most afraid of authority. They gave in once you demonstrated (using force) that you represented the side that invented all the sides. Packard used to tell Wentworth that there were better, equally effective ways. You worked it so you could screw the people who had real power. Man, did Packy hate them. What was that

Marine's name again?

Wentworth will never understand. He is whistling, "There's a yellow rose of Texas that…." and putting on his jacket so that he can go out and watch stuff.

Wentworth lazily took the elevator to the ground floor, leaning against the back wall, staring listlessly at the ceiling. A feeling of humanness and temporality was crawling around him in the flickering green light enclosed by paneled walls.

The street was noisy. Luke could feel hunger opening the sack-strings of his stomach again. Earlier he had thought that the meal at Poule's would last him through the day, but drinking always made him want to eat.

Walk or take the car? Wentworth had an apartment in Venice that he was loaning presently to a friend from the East whose father committed suicide a month ago. His pal was shaky and too spooky to hang around. Wentworth knew from going home the first few nights, Ed did nothing but go to bars and try to nail anything that moved. Ed thought to escape his plutocratic past by making himself into slime. Wentworth's sympathy had hit empty after ten miles with the guy. He decided to walk over to a nearby coffee shop, drink the black stuff, fill himself with bland sandwiches and desserts.

Out of the corner of his eye Wentworth could see a silver Jaguar pulling up next to him. In it sat Judith Poule looking snug and ready to make it with a weightlifter.

Substance, quantity, quality, relation, place, time, position, possession, activity and passivity—Wentworth tried to force an unembarrassed and sober smile to his lips. This immediately amused Ms. Poule because she thought (by the way Wentworth walked) that he liked to think himself a free agent and not someone's hired puppet. There was an omnific creaking from his shoes when Wentworth tilted forward to greet the dog lady. She was going to suggest going somewhere together. She's opening the passenger door and patting the seat with her hand, "Here, boy. *Wheee*!" Maybe if Wentworth thought of it from another perspective. It wasn't like meeting the wife after a day of work. She was always filled with tales of horror: Dora's kidney infection that had gotten worse, the cancer of the mouth that had put Phyllis' husband in the hospital for an operation had gone wrong, her therapist's arm been pierced by a straw in an Iowa tornado. He could get through this.

Well, anyway, he's already in the car, being offered a cigarette and being asked sporty questions about what he liked to do with his life when he wasn't chasing girls.

"They're not always girls." Wentworth protested. But breaking silence, triggered the trap. Ms. Poule paid for everything. At about three in the morning, Luke found himself again in the elevator, again on his couch with the phone at arm's length, but off the hook. He passed into sleep having found forgetfulness the easy way. He did not dream about anything except, maybe, the color of a dead body.

III. IN WHICH THE PHYSICIST IS TALKED TO

Professor Edgar Dranthus was reached after the frustration of finding parking, being misdirected by a well-meaning guard to chemistry building halls Luke ran to escape the formaldehyde smell. A fat associate professor in a fake polyester aloha shirt with palms bending into the breeze (or a tidal wave—you couldn't tell which) redirected him to the proper concrete face opposite the skin he was in.

Remembering the scientific faculty and staff at his own college, Wentworth conjured Dranthus as the usual untanned, spayed professor with a plump wife and seven healthy misdirected, but musically adept, offspring. The professor would be bald, white-shirted, and budding a paunch.

Dranthus looked as sharp as a cat's claw sitting behind his desk, his two feet up and shod in expensive running shoes, a formula on the blackboard behind him. Dranthus smiled a very carnivorous smile. Now, this was a suspect.

Wentworth looked at the tiger and the tiger looked quizzically back as if to say, "Me, a man eater? What makes you think so? It isn't this gigantic fang (Sprong! It comes out from behind thin black lips) is it?"

"You're here to see me about Alica Poule aren't you?" an insincerely paternal code of sounds purred.

"Yes. On her father's bequest. She's been missing three weeks now."

"A private dick, are you? Sorry about the jargon. I love those things."

"Who's your favorite?"

"I rampage through them all. Solution seeking and guessing are an obsessional habits of mine."

"Extension of the work?"

"Not really. Detective writers don't seem to know how to handle the mechanics very well. No Prousts or Pynchons. Suspense writers are better. Visually, like in Hitchcock."

Went was already lost. He didn't read. Did he look like a character in a book?

"What's that you're working on?" Wen pointed past Drathus at the blackboard.

"Heat transfer formula."

"Solar power?"

"Molecular structure. Biophysics. We want to see what happens when we can control growth rates in cells, regeneration, degeneration processes. Kind of like finding out if we could keep cows fat by feeding them half as much and still get good milk."

"Can you?"

"We could do lots of new things if older markets didn't dictate precedence."

W.W. wanted to pull back even further. "Did you know Alica very well?"

"We went out a few times. A fast girl—in every way. Wanted to absorb physics in the professor's bed."

"Did she learn much?"

"Well, she had to stand in line for awhile till I found out she was rich. Most of my students are affluent, but her dad's got this real estate hustle going. With all of those women. You know. That made me make a place for her nearer the top of the line."

W. looked at the beaming lighthouse bright grin. A fantasy world relating to a field he'd never imagined about swallowed him up.

"I haven't heard from or seen Alica in about six months. I like to fight, keep a constant contest going. But she'd hung around twisted artists for too long. The kind that spend years cranking up a few mediocre ideas and expect to stun the world with them. Didn't get along. I opened the gate and shooed her back to her autistic pastures."

Wentworth needed hosing down. He didn't know what he was looking at. His pauses didn't go unnoticed or undamaged.

"Is there anything else? Pardon me a sec." Dranthus turned round and changed a few figures of the formula on the blackboard. Mused before them. Said, "There you are!" before turning back to a withered Luke. "Anything else you want to know about the lost Diana?"

Insight wasn't that foreign to Luke and so he asked if Professor Dranthus knew either Professor Obolus, the economist, or Professor Boil. "Know Boil pretty well. We play squash together. Obolus belongs to the same club. He runs around the track a little and spends lots of time in the steam bath. He's about fifty and a fuddy-duddy. You'll find out, if you talk to him, that all he can talk about is 'his theory'. Did he know Alica Poule?"

"Apparently."

"What'd they do, play an exciting game of dominoes together?"

"Hey, this guy is vicious," Wentworth thought. But he overexaggerated.

"Would you like to join me for lunch?" the prickly physicist asked. Wentworth made it a question of where and it turned out to be the university cafeteria. The detective's stomach cringed as though its ears had just heard the tale of a bloodthirsty disaster or as though the eyes had just witnessed the decapitation of a beloved friend. Wentworth, you're turning into a stomach, I swear!

Luke remembered a pressing engagement. "Sorry. Have to keep going on this thing." Dranthus intrigued him and W. could have had a salad or some coffee while fascinating upon Dranthus' career, life, opinions. The stomach bugled its loyal citizens into the main square of the small cathedral town and ordered a fight be made to silence the whelping inside it. Wentworth snapped to attention, saluted the prime minister, and obeyed the imperial command.

Leaning comfortably back in the seat of his car and driving towards Chinatown, Luke canvassed his future prospects. They appeared, to his milky perception, not at all bad. The jobs he had gotten were all leading up to this, present, much better thing. Judith had made some promises about absorbing him into the company if things turned out well in the immediate instance.

Little sister was not all that much to worry about—in Ms. Poule's opinion. That morning, Luke's ex-wife, Ingrid, had called to complain about "their" daughter. In spite of the hostilities between them, the daughter was becoming more and more vivacious. The sorrow of her parents did not stop the bloom, nor the development of her figure. Barbara and Luke were quiet about Jenny, but had exchanged glances of unconscious half agreement that the girl would not be as easy to steer as previously thought. Going to college did not seem to appeal to the girl. Her former rapid brilliance in studies was falling behind in proportion to her budding. Wentworth suddenly remembered when last seeing her, how she had sprung up from the carpet watching the late movie and stretched her young body. Wentworth allowed his neck a shiver before having his attention diverted by a group of skateboarders headed off the curb out in front of him. He refused to slow and, as he passed the last one (who he missed by a wide margin), he got the finger.

This, miraculously enough, made him feel better. Death city. No need to have the urban blues because the kid isn't going to walk in the footsteps of … But Wentworth couldn't think of anyone pure or great who he'd like his daughter to be like. She was all right. The abuse she was suffering wouldn't hurt her. The bright sun would forget all about it. The smoggy sky would turn brown studies to gold. (What crap.)

Wentworth pulled into the parking lot of his favorite Chinese restaurant. Why had he been followed?

Two guys dressed like college students, and not professional muscle, were climbing out of a beige Cadillac with Texas license plates. They tried to approach casual and relaxed, not realizing it was those affects that made them obvious.

Wentworth hated warning/shakedown routines. He stood against the door of the car with his fingers searching to lift the cap off the mace in his coat pocket. He was having trouble with it. Here they come.

The shorter of the two was greasy, blond-balding and had a glazed and fixed opium blue stare to his ferrety eyes. Luke guessed that he would try the talking. The other fellow looked more killer-like, slack and even amused by his cohort's automaton's demeanor. The little guy fancied himself a slick tongue. They had on running shoes.

"Mr. Wentworth?" the scaggily one inquired.

"What's up, kid?" Went shot to tease, sting.

A qualifying pause of vehement indignation. The insulted voice suggested they talk somewhere in private.

"We'll talk where we stand."

"We're friends of Alica Poule's, Mr. Wentworth. We'd like to know if you've found where she might be."

"How did you know that I was looking for her?"

"Through her father."

Went bluffed. "You look like Dranthus butthole lickers to me. Followed me from the campus. So what's this really about?"

Wentworth took a punch to the stomach for his surmise, but had the mace out and spraying every which way before he could be hit again. Screams and curses. Or was that, curses and screams? Wentworth was in his car and driving off before his assailants could regain their gravity.

The punch in the stomach only increased his appetite. So, instead of doing anything sensible, he found a phone booth and called up Dranthus (who was out). He then drove back to the same parking stall.

The restaurant was in a minor uproar. First, these two kids, (one rubbed his eyes while screaming he was "Eatapuss," and now a woman who refused to vacate the ladies room because she accidentally flushed her dentures down the john.

The waiter was surprised by Luke's indifference. He gleefully ordered as though the world was not roaring and terribly upset.

After having satisfied his unnatural lusts, Luke again assaulted Dranthus' office number. Out.

He walked out into the easy sunshine of the unconcerned afternoon. Leaning on his car were his former friends, smiling in greedy expectation of beating him senseless.

Luke took one look, and about-faced back into the restaurant where he met the surprised features of the head waiter. He was still kicking his wits over what to do about the toothless fat lady in his toilet. Customers were deserting.

The two physics majors closed on the coward. At the front of the building they split up, one staying out front, the other to cover the back.

Wentworth anticipated this rather sophomoric plan and went into the men's room, helped the sexagenarian who was having trouble with his fly to vacate, then locked the door and crawled out the bathroom window.

The extremely impatient lord of quantum numbers waiting out front couldn't wait for his revenge upon Wentworth and deserted his post to find the chicken dick. Spying this, Wentworth, cackled and made a little blue-snake run for his car.

The balding, greasy-haired pseudo-gangster, Bobby, soon discovered that Wentworth's throat was not in the restaurant. He heard the head waiter complaining vitriolically about his second locked toilet door. A brace of policemen came in to liberate the locks. Bobby made a call. Two policemen escorted the babbling woman out of the toilet while Bobby and his cohort, John, sat down to eat. They figured Wentworth was about out of tricks—a brain his size couldn't go much further, they agreed. Next round, it would be Wentworth who would be losing his choppers.

Luke also had an appointment with the economist, Oscar Obolus, on the S.C. campus at three o'clock. He would be late if he had to go through the same tortuous search for the right building as before. Disgust was building cheap motels in his mind. Poule wanted his daughter back because of some heavy business deal. Judith Poule hated dad's tentacles and was trying to convince Luke to go slow, or even not go at all. Dranthus was a liar. Alica had something going on with him, and the other two, maybe ... Was this something other than the usual greased pole climbing contest played in the art community?

Wentworth's thoughts were beginning to shake him a bit. He

reached a hand into the glove compartment to slug down some gin. Luke was hoping the economist was as mousey as Dranthus described. If so, he would push for some answers.

Oscar Obolus was munching on the last of his lunch, a liverwurst and onion sandwich accompanied by a Coke and some carrot sticks. Luke rapped on the office door.

A burly voice bid, "Enter." Obolus' two hundred and twenty-two pound, ex-wrestler's nose was stuck into a turn of the century cambist. As soon as Wentworth saw Obo, he decided to abandon his belligerent "talk to me" attitude. Wentworth's conspiracy meter flung itself into the red.

"Ah, Mr. Wentworth. The boys just called. They say the Chinese food there," and here Obulus bit wolfishly into his liverwurst, "is really great."

These people, whoever and whatever they were, were in the superposition. Wentworth exhaled a sigh and slumped down into the chair facing the money man. The fact struck the detective that he was close to being pinned. Any question, even the simple ones, seemed evadable. His nose started to itch. Was he the donkey in this show? Step forward. Don't you see the carrot? Nope. It was Obolus' onions.

Obolus seemed to enjoy Luke's discomfort and did not bother to toy with the minimally catatonic detective.

Wentworth spied the real cause of his nose's irritation on a ledge atop Obolus' bookcase. An orange-striped Tom, gigantically fat, lying with forepaws lazily crossed for a headrest. Obolus began to assume a similar pose across the surface of his desk. Cat dander. Four green eyes chided Wentworth as he slipped around in his chair on a courageous hunt for a cigarette and a match.

Obolus began. "Do you know what happens in a natural system when the consumers begin to overshadow the producers?

Threaten the existence of the respiratory cycle of the producers through headless action, Mr. Wentworth?"

"The house goes broke. But statistically, probability-wise, I mean, that can't happen," Wentworth stammered after a moment of reflection.

"We're not playing a game of chance here, Mr. Wentworth."

"What is it then?"

"A mystery. False clues have been planted. Its heroes have been placed beyond love. An improbable set of circumstances must be tied up to satisfy the anxiety for order, neat remarks made about the many disfigured corpses."

"How late are we into this?"

"It's about over. Outside, lightning is about to strike and the power to fail."

"Where am I?"

"In my office, Mr. Wart. And it's your turn to try and spin an interesting web for me."

"I want to find Alica Poule."

"More and more I expect."

"Are you hiding her from me?"

Obolus shifted his head on his folded arms and looked up at the cat. "I've heard that Alica went to Rome with a bird-brained sculptor."

"The police have ascertained that she hasn't left the country."

"The police? Are they reliable?"

Wentworth was pulling the cart at a nice even pace by now. Realizing it, he stopped, but not to Obolus's surprise. Obolus stood up, walked over to the bookcase and lifted the cat down. He petted it behind the ears and stroked it under its chin with his thick forefinger.

"What's his name?"

"Jay. After Jay Gould."

"Gould tried to sell the country out, didn't he?"

"No, not really. He just tried to put too much cheese spread on the concrete. But seriously, Jay was exactly like the rest of us, only brilliant."

"You admire him, do you?" Wentworth tried some bait.

"Credit where it's due. Can I have your question now?"

Luke had played cat and mouse many times, and never ended up a jackass before. He had usually found at least one hole in the argument of the person he was shaking down by now. But this time? No holes. No logic. No arguments. He didn't mind playing the clodhopper for these profs. They'd give him what he wanted, or he'd tear their—

"What's on your mind, Wentworth!" Obolus purred. "I'm busy."

"Oh, forget it. You wouldn't tell me anything anyway. And, I've seen enough." Wentworth tromped out of the door wondering what to do.

Obolus put down the cat and gave a strange look to his unfinished sandwich. For a moment, Oscar's spinal column became a wedge of wet clay topped by a grey maraschino cherry.

The cat divorced him and by climbs and leaps regained his roost. The bird had flown too early because of some miscalculation of his. Edgar was going to be furious and, Aloysius, condescendingly amused.

Wentworth needed something. If he had been there, Luke would have gotten a great laugh out of the way Alica was toying with Aloysius over in his office. She was making fun of the Mobius strip gauntlet they were making the poor slob detective run. Imagine having to talk to dreary Dranthus or the obtuse Obolus for more than five minutes! They were each missing quantities as far as … Teasing Boil about his comrades delighted the sprite, but Boil only feigned inattention in order to make the girl stay lively. Her talents were singular, but she was a known quantity with a definite and limited purpose in the plot Boil was hatching. Her nervous animation was an attempt to escape the confines of the role that Boil was constructing around her. "Now, listen up," Boil was saying....

Wentworth was driving over to the Cal State campus to complete the triangle that Shirley had crowded into the day. As he pulled into the parking lot, Alica was leaving Boil.

Luke took one look at Boil and intuited he was dealing with someone stable. The professor wore all the right clothes, smoked a pipe, who quietly let trends pass. Boil didn't look like he would violate the young, and he certainly didn't appear like he had ever told a willful lie. Luke explained his search to the quite attentive Boil. Boil stated that he knew the girl well enough, that he'd seen her, oh, three weeks ago at a faculty party out at the marina. She seemed to have gotten over her infatuation with microbiology because she was back to having fun and not pouring over formulas she would never comprehend. Fun, at a faculty party? Luke thanked Boil for his time and excused himself.

He took a long breath in the hall, especially after inhaling some of the females going by, and swore, "The bastards are made out in triplicate."

IV. THE BIG DOGS ARE LAZY AND THE LITTLE DOGS ARE ANGRY

I f a man sets himself a task (Went was thinking about quitting this case) and starts off trying to skate a straight line to its goal, he'll soon find himself taking lefts and rights (to the chin and the temple) that leave him dazed/amazed at the amount of plotting going on in the surrounding lanes.

Those in life who are interested in piling up money or power don't want anything else in life regarded as better than what they're after. Lovers of the passionate transitory or the ineluctable modality of the diaphanous, do you sneer? Well, nothing's too difficult if you're prepared to be wicked. Wentworth is saying things to himself about the experiences of the last few days and dedicating himself to shutting these thinkers down.

Luke drove off the campus in disgust. Phone. Phone. Cellular phone? Not yet. Wentworth pulled up across from a pizza place to call Poule and report. Through the large front window of the eatery, he could see a fight between a bearded black and a slob in a t-shirt. The seated wife was tugging at her husband's arm. The arriving pizza ended up in the black man's beard and face. He pulled a gun and smeared the construction worker's brains across the room. The wife jumped up and bit the man's arm. He tried to shake her off before anyone could surround and grab him. But, actually, the place emptied and they were struggling alone. Finally, he managed to shoot her in the leg, just below the knee. This folded her to the floor. The man wrapped napkins around his bleeding forearm. It was too late. A black and white arrived and demanded the man's surrender. He made a move to use the woman as a hostage. He lifted her from the floor for a shield. She was too heavy to support with his disabled arm and she slipped out of his grip back to the floor. A cop shotgunned him as he started to back away from the front window. Poule's line was busy. Luke tried it five more times until someone answered. He put in a report to the secretary about the day's atrocities. An ambulance arrived. Then two. Then three.

It began to rain. Wentworth's internal tides were swelling to the point of wanting to smash the wall of deceit obstructing his view. He had a momentary flash. Judith was Poule's gorgeous pair of feelers. He walked dissolutely back to take the wheel of his less than sun-dragging car.

"Astonish me. Be astonished," the pavement proclaimed. "Everything is a miracle."

Before Luke could put the key into the ignition, he thought back on his undergraduate days. He'd spent all his extra time in bars. What has he gotten out of that? He remembered the panic he felt the first time he got it in the back of a car with the clit queen. Lost his wallet. Going back for it, he discovered her going down on his best friend. Then he felt ordinary. And in feeling ordinary, inferior. (Now, he would assemble a chorus to sing perpetual praise to such an innocent babe.)

These people couldn't make him feel a failure like that again, could they? He was thirty-five and not nineteen. He drank French wines and fornicated in freedom. "Why is there always so much more to everything?" he moaned as he headed back to the office playing H's *Water Music*. The future's uncertain, but the final scene's clear. A downpour began to slow the traffic. Wentworth grabbed the bottle from the old glove compartment and ran its contents down the street of his throat.

A police siren wove its way through the cross pattern of motorized metal. He shoved the bottle between his legs and steered over to the curb. The scream passed. At this hour, there were very likely desperately stupid minds set on knocking off a corner liquor store. Strange unions. Conceptions. Outside the usual order. Spaceships rowing softly home through the atmosphere to pick up the quickly damned, saving them from destined future generations of ceaseless struggle. What was that? Back into to glove compartment with you, chump.

Drunk. He was taking lefts and rights back to home base. What would he find there? He dreaded. In hopes of hearing of Alica Poule's body floating in the marina harbor, Wentworth turned on the radio. "Terrorists have taken over the nuclear reactor outside New York City and are making demands for as many millions of dollars as there are people in the state." Wentworth turned it off. If you hear about it, it's happened. If you haven't heard about it, the chances are that by the time it's over, it doesn't matter that it happened at all. Too late. The radio had caught him shitfaced with its report.

Wentworth considered stumbling up the steps to his office, but opted for the elevator. One minute before coming down the hall to his office, Bobby and John (who had waited for three hours) had stepped across the street for a bite to eat. They had discussed whether Wentworth would show precisely when they were out. They decided that if he came in, they would see him from the coffee shop and could go right back to get him. Worthless had to take a desperate leak, so he forwent the lights and stumbled to the toilet.

Shirley was taped to a chair the boys had moved into the bathroom. Naturally, she was gagged and quite passive by this time. She bitched and screeched "I quit" while Wentworth fussed to release her. He started to rip the tape off of her hairy arms.

Men's minds are constantly cheating on them. Throughout Shirley's whimpers and shrieks, his thoughts were at the race track. What horse would win Belmont? How long before there was another horse that could make the Triple Crown? He wanted to be in a poker parlor among some shrewd fifty-dollar-a-day regulars or on a plane for Vegas. Aging showgirls dressed in gaudy red and spangles appealed to him. Kid's and men's faces seemed to cluster around him.

"Oh Luke, please. They made fun of my fat and poked me with blackjacks!"

Wentworth got a pair of binoculars from the bottom desk drawer and had a look. John left the coffee shop to put money in the meter. Different car from the one earlier. Luke conjectured it was stolen and called the police. He'd just seen his best friend's car hiked at such and such an address by two … And here he gave a description. Being the good friend he was, he knew the car's individuating flaws—even its license plate number. The two schoolboys were soon dragged away by plainclothesmen.

Shirley was grateful and happy upon hearing Luke's report about what had happened to the two inconsiderate amateurs. She accepted Wentworth's apologies. Now that the danger had been neutralized on the speeding train of her life, Shirley bathed in the milk of her revenge and re-devoted herself to job and justice.

"I'm so glad it's over," she sighed.

"Over?" Luke smirked. "Over for tonight."

Where was her ring? Had they taken her ring. Ring! Answer the phone. Went stooped over and followed the possible path of a loose ring falling from a flabby finger. He found it. Ring! It was Poule, returning his call.

"Is my daughter all right?"

Luke told a story about a shooting on the campus. Alica's cycle was supposed to be at its peak for the month. Poule could not understand how she could even come near a shooting. Poule said he'd recheck the computer forecast. She had to be found soon, though. He needed her before her predicted crash. It always came within a few days after her peak.

Shirley left satisfied. Luke went for a bottle in another pocket of the desk. The binoculars stared at him from the owl-eyed end, making him look distant and miniature to the license hanging on the opposing wall. Is irony (an arm of thought) a perverse limb that must agonize pleasure? Naw.

Room spinning around him, Luke saw the "way." The interminable design of a lunatic insect. Monotony swizzled the juicier intents of the inner discontented claw that allured the drunken, boatless boy. Wentworth remembered the New England summer thundershowers and what it was like to be seven and sail makeshift craft down the streams headed for the end of the hill's gutter. The enthusiasm and energy that could go into such an activity! It was everything removed from studying books, fighting with the siblings, or thinking up ways to cut chores. The raincoat was? A smooth cadmium yellow. A fisherman's hat came with it. The snaps, brass. And in the rain, the things lost the tortuous factory smell.

Take another drink, Luke. It's the memory prison. Guards prowl the hallways shouting names: Newark, New Salem, Deep

River, Lincoln, Dorothy Provine, Pleasant Valley, Orange, The End of Time.

A dog seemed to bark as the words passed by in their black uniforms. Passion makes one think in a circle. Circle the coarse brawl, the dainty den, the crude benevolence of a disordered life. Have another drink, Wentworth. The Amazon's plants are the lungs of the earth. They may be cut out. Ugliness is the one reality. What you need is forgetfulness. Sing out the hopeful degenerate's song.

Luke's head was crossing into that clear zone where thoughts assume independence from the mind they have ostensibly sprung. The identity is not reducible, defines itself (some little "what") by the accumulation of its choices. "Wentworth is cheating himself," the arcing voices that surround him are saying. "Wentworth needs to reevaluate what has happened today." He knows more has happened than he has a handle on. Handle, calculate, decipher those messages you've been receiving, Mr. Demon.

The mind, alive in the crippled body. Wentworth ticks off possible permutations and possible forms hidden behind some of the less obvious props of the day's happenings at an undetectable rate. The shopkeeper is beginning to discuss the price of character with Wentworth. He wishes to stop the talk while he still understands everything, before he passes out. No.

V. JUDITH POULE IN HER TUB (AFTER THE 'LUDOVISI THRONE')

Venus holds unending court. Judith Poule murdered the afternoon by playing tennis with a potential client and now she's at home pushing her sweaty, tight little white uniform into a wicker hamper. While the servants draw the bath water, checking to make sure it's right with a thermometer, Judith puts some powder up her nostrils and tires her sensuating body with a gin martini.

"It's ready now, Miss." Judith leans on the houseboy's shoulder and he leads her to her bath. He leaves and a maid comes in to help Judith out of her silk, amber-orange colored, striped housecoat and into the water.

Judith likes lines from the Bible read to her while she's soaking in the tub; movie reviews, or world news. The Cubans amuse her. She's been to Africa a few times. Judith has the maid scrub her. She kisses the maid. Judith helps the maid undress. The maid slips into the tub. This happens every day. Judith Poule cannot find enough. The maid wonders why she has to stay a maid. Judith grabs the maid's brains and tosses them into a wok of questions about what's on the menu tonight.

VI. AT THE DESK IN A DRUNK AGAIN

Some folks find glory in their birth, others in their skill, their wealth, their bodies' force. Went gives himself up to dream, hoping they'll give him what life in the visible world won't. He's a silly reed. This time, I won't bother you with what he's dreaming. Just remember that he's asleep at his desk while forces are massing to manipulate him more vigorously.

VII. IN WHICH DRANTHUS, OBOLUS AND BOIL MEET

The three flowers met in a Taco place to feed Obolus' craving for secrecy and burritos. Dranthus hated the stuff and wouldn't drink beer—the only alcohol served. Boil liked everything. While Dranthus was an elitist, feeding himself on snobbery, and Obolus was a middle term, satisfied with slobbery, Boil enjoyed every sensation without reluctance. Dranthus mistrusted him because he played too much. When the government had cut off the funds for his research once, Dranthus made demands and, after they were not met, he quit. Obolus had always been an institution man. He never worked problems with student help. They distracted his attention, ruined his concentration. Boil was a floater and could probably work effectively with a jackhammer raving five feet from him. The man's screens were impenetrable. Boil's wife was the only one who ever had bothered him, but she had died a year ago of cancer.

Dranthus never witnessed the horrors (especially in the last dying days) she could make her husband feel with only a movement of her eye or the quick strike of her reptilian tongue.

Obolus was gay (Wentworth finally perceived) and this revolted Dranthus. This might subject Oscar to blackmail, and that liability Dranthus' diligent mind didn't want mucking up the plan. Boil saw all weaknesses as negative strengths. Obolus' mind was lost legitimate, published material and new ideas didn't bother him. The brilliant analysis that Obolus had made of rising economic social systems and structures from the time of the guilds to the multi-national dealings of the Krupps and Wittgensteins, didn't serve as a model for any of the "changes" that they ultimately had in mind. Boil had been told to keep an eye on Obolus. This he did by indulging the enthusiast and including him in on some of the peripheral scenes. This made Obolus feel secure. To him, these tidbits were gargantuan. It amused Boil and, oppositely, disgusted Dranthus.

Obolus was on his sixth burrito. Dranthus was anxious about his two students in jail. Could they send in a fourth party, someone untraceable, to bail them out? Boil made a fuss, "Hell, this taco shell's hard and cold." While rearranging the onions, tomatoes, lettuce and cheese inside of it, Aloysius forwarded the opinion that those two dumb little clucks were safer where they are.

"What were they doing in Wentworth's office?"

"Trying to find out what information the detective already had on them in his files."

"What? That dry old wad of crusty gum doesn't know squat. Why is your paranoia so rampant, Dranthus?"

Does it have anything to do with the rainy weather? Are you so far gone as to think that a puppy private eye searching for Alica Poule's hot tail is actually capable of memorizing a fifty digit, thirty-step problem from a blackboard? The dick probably didn't know what a function or a derivative is much less the use of a Poisson Bracket. "Dranthus, your problem is…." Boil broke off here to chomp on the taco and push the matter that had missed going down, dangling from his mouth, in with a nudge of his thumb … "You want to know everything. You're creating reactions more dangerous than the untested thing."

Obolus nodded, his full mouth, in agreement and almost opened it to add a syllable to what Boil was forewarning but he caught himself. The sight of a half masticated roll of slop might chase the intended victim into a fury about "what manners were" and Obolus would never get his barb in.

Before Obolus could swallow, Dranthus was already up and ranting about loyalty. "My two boys deserve consideration."

Obulus and Boil can see Dranthus getting behind the wheel of his green-blue Continental, fuming and fumbling with the safety belt, trying to silence door buzzers and roll out of his space without incident, and they laugh at him, mouths wide open and full of refried beans.

Boil was thinking about how good it was to have Obolus around to taunt and torture Dranthus with. Obolus was asking his stomach if it could tolerate another burrito. Would Boil like another beer? He was going up to the counter to put in a small order. Boil wanted two beers. Obolus was pleased to the ends of the earth that his chief was going to get drunk. What divine majesty it must be to be so sure of your horse that, even if you drop the reins for a few miles, you'll still be travelling safely in the same direction when you wake. Boil was a god! A god. And Obolus was his friend! Oh, boy, Oscar!

Boil was glad Obolus was easy to please. He never got drunk on beer but liked to put on an act, even pretend he was loose-lipped and dropped confidences to eager-eared patsies. "The bigger the boob, the harder you twist his tail," was Boil's formula. Here comes Obolus back to get stung. Boil grins like a chess-playing ten year old who's just realized that.

VIII. BECAUSE OTHER THINGS HAVE REFUSED TO HAPPEN, A BRIEF REPORT ON W.W.'s DREAM

Wentworth dreamed that he was being dragged on the end of a tether around a central point through smooth, inky black water, just ahead of a ravenous shark. The shark became a bear. The water turned into land, a forest. The tether disappeared and Wentworth ran through the low shrubs, across streams, and through thick and thin trees. He stopped to look over his shoulder once, but there was the bear. The bear did not become anything else. At one point Wentworth ran across a super highway, but something dictated he leap across like a deer and not hunt for help from a passing car.

Wentworth woke in a sweat, sorry that he had not gone to the library. He wanted to know why those three were together. What could Alica Poule's interest in Obolus be? What did they have in common? They must have published. What did they do? Wentworth was slightly ashamed for not wondering more about Alica. They had her. Why did they have her? Wentworth tried to close his eyes. There was the bear! "Open. Open sesame, eyes."

Oh damn! He'd almost slept through it! Tonight was his poker night. Having won an unusually large sum from his playing partners last week, they were sure to think that he was skipping out to avoid vengeance. Luke scribbled a note to himself about going to the library. Two notes. He left one on the desk and shoved the other into his pocket.

This week the game was at Hans Eagan's house, a place up behind the Hollywood Bowl. Eagan was an advertising man who pushed movies. Anything from "bring your barf bag to this one, folks" to intergalactic spectaculars.

Hans and Luke were the two most familiar faces at the game. Everyone else's fortunes fluctuated more than theirs. Also, when neither Eagan or Wentworth were down, they didn't care about sinking a few feet lower. It was only when it was obvious that some new phiz wasn't going to accept apologies for lack of cash and that maybe a gun was locked in the glove compartment of his car, that Eagan and Wentworth bowed out playing hands they couldn't cover.

Wentworth was feeling lucky and was about to lock the door when Poule called. Demanding. Demanding very emphatically to see the boy immediately. Now what was this going to be about? Luke made sure he had his mace and went whistling down the stairs.

When he got to Poule's, a servant escorted him to the garden. The tether was tied to Wentworth again. Did he see it? Luke leaned over the illuminated fishpond. Irises lifted their flowered stalks above the water. Petals the color of sandstone vases, blood-purple enamel, blue-flamed with ochre orange, their calyxes, twisted and sulphureous. The water lilies and nelumbos held out their fainting blossoms that were splayed by gravity and buoyed by the boundary of the water.

Luke noticed a bell on the ledge of the fishpond. He softly began to tinkle it. The power of a feeding signal! The carp in the pool stopped their circumrotating and formed themselves into a wedge. It came and stopped directly before the jar of pellets resting on the flagstones.

Luke refused to feed them, waited to see how long before they returned to their endless stroll. It was for only few seconds. As they moved away, Wen rang again and back they shot. The tether. He fed, they devoured.

Wentworth was still watching, in particular, an enormous golden carp whose snout rose above the water and seemed to be asleep, when Poule appeared. He didn't seem as angry as he had been on the phone, "Sorry to have you drive all the way over. False alarm. The police found someone they thought was Alica."

"Why the anger over the phone?"

Poule grimaced, "That was fright, Mr. Wentworth. The police were asking if a corpse found on Topanga Beach was my daughter."

Luke showed spontaneously that he felt like a complete imbecile for having misgivings about Poule.

"It's all right," Poule reassured. "Go home and sleep. Get a fresh start in the morning."

Deuces, Diamonds, Straights, and Queen High-Straights disappeared into a black bottomless hat. Luke heard himself saying that he had been ready to call it a day when Poule called. Jack offered Luke a bed for the night, a sauna, and a rubdown by a "damn wonderful" masseuse. Luke worked his way out of the invitation by a simply splendid set of twists and crouches Houdini would have admired.

The game! The game! Wentworth hardly wondered where Judith was tonight. Had he looked up at the second story, he might have caught sight of an arm moving a martini glass around. The lipstick on its edges smiled.

For a second, the plant blossoms in the lily pond seemed as exciting and intense as a woman's breathing flesh, but Went let the secret pass so that the L.A. night could fold him into her deck.

It occurred to Wentworth that nothing in the world would faze, much less "frighten" Jack Poule. Wentworth reflected on what the actual purpose of the phone call and the visit might have been. At Eagan's door, he let the thought drop. He was not playing well. Packard had always been very careful to avoid becoming a sap. Luke avoided pratfalls by mostly staying off the stage. His cases were usually too innocuous to make him the cut-out in some ambitious plan. Luke dismissed the unnerving notion that he may have overstepped himself. He tried on the thought that maybe he, too, could be clever. The cards might be good tonight and, unfortunately, they were.

When Luke got back to his office he found it ransacked. What was he supposed to have? Who wanted it? The library note was missing, so it was the Poule case. There really hadn't been fifty terms and thirty steps in Dranthus' equation. Luke had gotten most of it. Scrambled, though. Wentworth didn't learn enough calculus. He knew functions and differentials though, and from looking up the symbol in a text, he'd soon know what those brackets did.

Application is everything. Apply here, apply there. Wentworth would never figure it out from the formula. Dranthus must have published work. What he did five years ago was probably still close to what he was doing now.

What had Luke been doing five years ago? Not what he was doing now. He'd done what paid right over the table and then got taxed. Tonight it had come to him in so much more beautiful forms. Would pretty ladies paired with knaves, nines and kings net him profits? Luke stared at the husked office and turned his back on it. Tonight he could afford? Eagan's game or? He drove over to the medical technologist's apartment. She came to the door after several rings, but wouldn't let him in. She was with someone else. "It was his own fault," she whispered raspingly. Luke looked rather fine to her, in a winner-killer mood. Closing the apartment door quietly behind her, she took Luke's forearm and led him around the corner of the building, away from the lights. Standing up was one of the young woman's favorite positions. It brought back her high school days and the night outdoor smells.

After about a half-hour of this, they went down to the pool, and water-mated for awhile. She'd only tried this first time the week before. She hadn't been wet enough, but tonight was fine.

Wentworth still didn't have a place to sleep and by now was exhausted. The nearest place from here was his Venice Beach place. He headed for coffee at an all-night grill first.

In the bizarre light of the shop, W. heard a wind rasp over a cool ridge inside a chamber of his heart. Caffeine? Went's waitress was rapaciously vivacious, talked in a private pandemonium about spooks and knocks to some bored cops and was generally off. W's mood was foul after having to overhear about the clusters of beasties that had tried to invade her bed. Had Luke suspected he was headed for the worse upon a shore of stranger woes, he would have gone back to his dismantled office.

IX. WHY FATHERS SHOULD NOT COMMIT SUICIDE AFTER THEIR SONS ARE GROWN

L uke found Ed in bed with a three hundred and fifty pound wino. Ed was passed out on top of her and she was moaning a little and wriggling to get her drunken fingers around the skinny top of a gallon jug.

Wentworth stepped up behind Edward and leaning across the base of the cherry wood bed, pulled Ed off. Luke wanted the kid out of his place. He couldn't shake him awake and worse yet, the woman started to scream at Wentworth about the private, beautiful act of love that he was violating by his belligerent presence.

This outburst greatly annoyed Wentworth. Ed, in a moment of creativity, had put Wentworth's silk sheets on the bed. Now they reeked almost as badly as if they had been smeared with liquid animal filth. He dropped Edward on the floor. A small grunt of complaint left the collapsed adventurer's lip. He folded mutely atop the barf stained bear rug. Wentworth proceeded to assault the fortress of fat who clung so greedily and shrieked so loudly into the ear of the near empty gallon.

Wentworth pried the juice out of her hand and threw it out the open window. The woman abandoned the bed upon seeing Luke's gun handle briefly expose itself from under his jacket. He was only a few chemical surges away from considering mutilation and (awk!) a burial of her various parts in the wet sand. Her insight was indeed deep. As she grabbed her frock, apologies drooled from her lips about seducing his mildly mad friend. Was the whole world doomed to perpetual chaos for fault over one trick apple?

Wentworth stripped the bed and threw the sheets out the window. He pulled the bear rug from under Ed and it followed. Luke didn't want to look at any of the rest of the place. He'd see a mess like the one at the Ashton sisters'.

The Ashton sisters, Sara and Meta, had lived in Luke's home town. At age sixteen, Luke became hot to own his first car and earned money every way he could. He'd sold seeds door to door, delivered papers, mowed lawns, painted fences, and had twice worked for the Ashtons.

Sara Ashton played the organ in church and was a heavy tippler. She always performed brilliantly through the first seven or eight bars before starting to slur the notes. First a little out of recognition. To the degree, that if you didn't know about her playing, you questioned your own ears. Then, a turn more radical. The score was on the rack and the notes screamed. Since the Ashton family had always generously supported the deity, no one complained much and the programs were merci-fully short. In her later years, Sara usually passed out before she had a chance to slip the torture in, so people accepted the program as "better."

Meta was, secretly, the town poet. Her sonnets to the lilacs and hawthorns of spring have recently come to light and are being dissected for possible comparisons to E.D., though there are none. Meta had always been hunched and in late age, it became her.

The Ashtons kept forty cats. None of the males were neutered, so that the creatures had to be kept apart. Wooden cages lined each side of the room, the males on one side, the females on the other, just like at a chaperoned junior high school dance. Each sex was let out separately to exercise, romp, play, and amuse the Ashtons.

Well, lick my hot light! The first time Luke got to know what went on inside the sisters' house, he came to install an air conditioner. Walking through the front door was more cataclysmic than walking into Fritz Lieber's cheese store in the middle of summer. The ladies were installing the cooling unit, three units actually, to overcome the complaints that some of the humane society people were making about the smells leaking out of the Ashton house. (On warm summer nights with light breezes, the Ashton name floated around.)

It had become progressively more difficult for the two aging ladies to care for the cats. Summer was returning and, already, the "talk" was stronger than ever before. Sara, who still showed up on Sunday for church, was hiding the fact that Meta had gone insane. What shame that would have brought upon the family! She had Meta tied to a chair, and sometimes gagged her. Oh. That's what some of those noises were. Not cat calls at all. Meta shouting her verses while wriggling in her chair.

Meta proved to have the stronger constitution. With all the extra work Sara had to do, she succumbed deeper to the grain and fell down the church stairs after an almost complete performance of "Nearer My God to Thee." The pastor and assorted townsfolk rushed to comfort the other bony sister.

No one really ever walked too close to the Ashton house

anymore and, one lovely woman fainted when the sheriff opened the Ashton front door. The cats had not been looked after well in the last six months. Sara could not clean cat boxes and take care of her sister too, so she had resorted to putting newspaper on the floor for the cats to do their duty. This explained to the always curious townspeople the mystery of why the two sisters ordered the big Boston Daily even though neither of them liked, particularly, to read.

Most of the cats were skinny and starving and were punctiliously gassed. Meta was untied, for it was at first thought that this abominable cruelty was some kind of drunken revenge of the one sister upon the other. When Meta tried to "*fitt-fitt nee-roww*" jab the minister's eye out with one of her very long and overgrown fingernails, it was decided that Meta was "gone."

The town kept on raising the reward for anyone who would clean out the Ashton sty. Wentworth volunteered when the offer went up so high that others began to consider it.

Luke was bright enough to obtain a surplus gas mask, but the odor saturated his pores and he had to go hiking in the mountains for a week (gas mask on most of the time because even he couldn't stand himself) after accomplishing the awful feat.

Wentworth recalled those days. And also others when, after staying out and rowdying at a bar, he was able to reach his bedroom and collapse next to his, then, pretty young wife, wearing, in a delightful pose, a violet-white nightgown. But Luke's mind went "*ffftt*" before he could continue. Damn Ed's father. What a mess! He snored the night into Ed's left ear.

X. WHAT OTHERS MAY BE THINKING WHILE LUKE SLEEPS

Different branches of every tree (the scientific, the cultural, overall mental) develop unevenly. Some of us are capable of being instruments of fantastic sensitivity, others of us are bird calls on flights through an indefinable flux. But, at some time or another we share a common jackhammering base from which no amount of thought, reflection, or motion can free us. Here we are, in bed with Time and Death.

Dranthus has the DT's tonight. He's celebrated the finding of the figures he's been searching for for five years. Now that he had them assembled, of course, a party. That was earlier. He's in bed with two remarkably beautiful students. Dranthus is thinking he could be Achilles in a war poem about the planet's destiny. Where to find a poet though, who could sing such a long five year song or be in his brain while the tides of deduction and perception comingled and, step by step, grain by grain, forged ... Oh, forget this. Right now D's mind is an obnoxious id-pile. It's impossible to like people who proclaim themselves, even when they are great. Why bother to explain Dranthus when he's only a miniature Macedonian prince, anxious about the talents of his father.

Boil is at home. He was at the party too, and even showed encouragement and excitement over Dranthus' success at the right times. Once, they had a private somber moment, justification begging approval, while they waited in the hall for the bathroom to empty. It took quite awhile, and so Dranthus had a chance to talk the miracle dead before the porcelain throne vacanted. Boil felt sorry for him. Dranthus' eyes glared at the Venus who emerged. But he forgot about his bladder and followed her down the hall anyway.

Boil was amused by everything his comrades in arms wanted.

He knew today could be yesterday, tomorrow. It all repeated, over and over and over again. There might be a brief great stir in the intellectual community if Dranthus' formula flew. In about 380 B.C., Democritus of Abdena had elaborated an "atomic theory." Democritus was also a too voluminous writer on science and understood the powers of seeds, plants and fruits. A brute time then and now. Dranthus believed that the world was in a final stress. This made Boil's soft flesh happy. A hysterical snigger. He poured himself a long drink. Gin. It infrequently gave him a hangover. Boil had only had the DT's once, as a graduate student celebrating his shift from the university's limited lab to a gigantic one owned by a corporate Morlock.

Boil hated mechanics and Dranthus was a mechanic. His formula was the fastest thing on the strip. See it describe the rings around Saturn! See it get old and rock on the porch with a sear on its hand from a slip of the dinner knife, one quarter of an inch deep. But it will be proven wrong. It will die. Maybe a footnote's worth in a more arcane magazine. He'll put it on antibiotics to keep it alive. That'll be your life's work, "D" for "debilitated."

Boil's world was bitterly alive. He showered, put on a pair of amethyst pajamas, set the alarm, loved danger (even though so little of it was directed against him). He slept like a prophet, naming the faces in the multiple wheels of probability and chance. Then, he parted the sea.

Judith Poule had no trouble doing anything and she disappeared from that window we last saw her behind to drive to a friend's house and look at some his paintings. The paintings were lousy. She insulted him and left to see another friend, a potter. Bob, the potter, was in the shed, blowing glass. Judith watched. A close musician friend was getting married. Bob was ladling out the blobs from the oven to zip-zip, crimp, fold, smooth into wine glasses. Judith left after half an hour and got into her former agent's bed.

That's enough about these characters. If you want to know about Poule, all he does is answer telephones from ten in the morning until two at night. The "big-picture" changes hourly and Poule's is always riding its trail. It may interest you to know what I'm thinking. Really, nothing at all. Today I was told about what it was like being female, desirable, eighteen and living in the Bahamas. I was shown brochures that were arriving in the mail to lure the now older, and already puffy, professional. The French International Club showed that the children could come along. Besides the sun and beach, skits and plays would be organized, minds and bodies shared in a spirit of rigorous Epicurianism. The brochures advertising American pleasures offered the individual experience, mating with younger, or even younger still, native women. Straight hedonism, no chaser. I wanted to go. The one, the many—it's confusion.

And, my, what a moral sewer I'm into.

Wentworth's nostrils got up to the smell of fried potatoes. Ed was cheery and full of questions for Luke. For example, "Have you ever done it with men? What did it feel like? Did it feel like…?"

Wentworth answered, "No," and Ed shut up for awhile and plopped some more mustard on his eggs. In Europe they ate French fries with mayonnaise—did Luke know that? They sold French fries and wursts from kiosks, usually near magazine stands. What did Luke think about the German newspapers, Stern and Bunte Illustriete? Isn't it funny the way the Germans have that obsession about always touching up the teeth by giving them that plaster enamel look? And always some sort of sun-bunny woman on the cover, while on the inside it's invariably a diet of stories about mass murder or stolen photographs of topless celebrities. What are you interested in, Luke? You haven't ever been to Europe, have you?

Luke piled some of the greasy potatoes onto the end of his fork and flipped them onto Ed's white shirt. Ed became catatonic. Luke thought about tying him to the chair and sitting him out for the incoming tide. But Ed's mother knew where he was and sent money. If the checks weren't cashed there'd be trouble. Mom would have Wentworth's ass gobbled if anything happened to sonny. It was all right for Ed to be sick. Sick people can be put back together nicely, if they're rich. The social class Edward was going to return to would "accept" the fact that he had gone over the edge. They all had at one time or another. It was a softball game, cocktail party conspiracy that they kept going for one another, even if you had to go "away." Wentworth was through staring at the frozen wonder child. What could he do to throw the switch back on? "Ah, forget it!" "O.K.," Ed replied.

Wentworth tuned on the car radio to the classical station as he pulled out onto the Pacific Coast Highway.

XI. IN WHICH WENTWORTH FINDS THE ENERGY OF THE FUTURE

T he library had a computer that could locate any book or article ever written, on shelves anywhere in the country. Dranthus had been pulled into the University of California system as soon as he had graduated from Harvard. Early on, Dranthus had been in astrophysics and had only moved over to atomic physics after his researches in radio spectronomy had led him into the fusion fun.

Dranthus' name was fairly everywhere from articles entitled, "What is a Controlled Fusion Reactor" for the consumption of the non-science interested public to more detailed analysis of the quest through works entitled, "Nuclear Fusion Reactions, Energy Balance Considerations, Theory of Binary Reactions; Reaction Power Density; (*thrillers*, all of them), The Reaction Free Path-Energy Division, Friend or Foe; Phenomena in a Completely Ionized Gas; The Longitudinal Confinement Problem Through the Pinch Instability Factor; Superconductions and Their Similarity to Plasma Oscillations Under

Thermonuclear Heat Pressures; Diffusion Across a Magnetic Field." And the list went on.

Luke found some of Dranthus' later articles were in the library. He scrambled to the information desk to get them before anyone else got the chance to check them out. Actually, he strolled. The pockmarked assistant arrived with a stack and Luke retreated to a corner. Eyes stared at him looking for a chair in the reading room. He raced a girl for the last one. Luke hated libraries very easily. He had met his wife in the college library, where he was working to raise money for a vacation to Mexico, which turned into a trip to the altar. She had been looking for Shelley and this immediately made Wentworth confident and superior. It was Keats and no one else for him at the time. His arrogance faded when he stared too long at her tight rear bending to lift the martyr from the bottom shelf. A date was arranged while she was holding the "great poet" (in Luke's words) firmly against her ample protrusions.

Luke's place was next to a man asleep who had been reading a science fiction book with a drawing of a tentacled female thing on the front and a photo of the mad looking, long nosed author on the back—bald with perpetual five o'clock shadow who looked like a coffee zombie.

Another misperception. It was almost immediately apparent that the scientific community once founded days, on the philosophy of advancement based on achievement and merit had degenerated into warring factions over whose methods and theories were best, not even best—to be pursued. They were fighting for the same short funds: cancer researchers, militant grandmothers, angry minorities. The halcyon days were buried and no fertility god was going to jump up and start singing about whose ideas should be sprung and whose chopped off at the stem. "Wonderful!" old sourpuss Wentworth thought (his romantic side popped out of his shirt front with the face of a gorgon and giggled).

Dranthus appeared to have lost his faith in the democratic system of having all concerned parties have their say. Time jerked by and nothing done. Everyone talked and no one did. Scientists were becoming no better than fat-cat Chaucer professors in their three hundred and seventeenth year of dismembering the anti-church hatchet man.

Luke laugh woke the science fiction fan. "Christ! You dog! I was dreaming the most fantastic adventure on Venus and your hee-hawing woke me up just three seconds before a life-fulfilling climax."

Wentworth pointed disdainfully at the old crock's fat and awake trouser worm. This belittled, silenced and embarrassed the complainer—to Wentworth's supreme satisfaction. "Better not drop back off pal," Luke warned, "because as soon as you do, I'll be there waiting in full executioner's regalia to lop off your miserable little head." The reader went red-faced and threw the paperback at Luke's chest. He let the book hit him and thud to the floor. The reading room had thirty-one indignant and curious eyes fixed on what action Luke would reciprocate with, but Wen only turned, surveyed the room, and wheeled himself away.

It was time for lunch. He thought he'd had it all figured out. Dranthus, Obolus, and Boil—crusaders for a new world order, sent by the popishly higher cause of science to free the world of the yoke the failing economic systems. Alica Poule was in on the conspiracy somewhere. Maybe she'd decided to back out. Possible.

She was probably like other kids, wanted revenge on mommy and daddy, but when it came to realizing that a few more billion people than that were to be snuffed, an excuse to run. Where should he go for lunch? Wentworth couldn't decide. He was so happy to be on the beam again, and so fast.

Some people are paying so much attention to the flesh that they never have trouble remembering that they don't have it for long. Others see only the fact that the flesh is mostly sad and never look up from their funk to the night, the sea or the sun behind it. First or last looks, either way, don't help the heart decide where to hop, up or down what pole. But the stomach! Following the stomach, the arms and legs take it.

 Obviating the constant vanity or displeasure involved in regarding our the basic position. Upside down. Gravity. Our own or the one created by the unmilkable way. Holds us down, though not back.

I don't want you to get the idea that Wentworth is a walking Pavlovian stomach, so while he is on the steps contemplating soul food or Thai, let me show you the three nasty fellows who are waiting around the corner for Wentworth by his car. They are not shy, dumb, or trying to figure out Wentworth. They are not looking soft core and student-like. They do not look like members of a crime organization, police detectives, or F.B.I. The three chameleons playing around Wentworth's car could not be mistaken for killers.

Upon deciding that the Mexican chili down the block would appease the demanding monster from within, Luke set off.

Luke's executioners grew tired of waiting and one was sent to locate him in the innards of the library. It was soon established that he'd left the library and wandered off. The three debated that (a) "The guy's been tipped off," (b) "Flaw. Somehow he's gotten wise," (c) "He's probably taking a walk thinking about what he's uncovered and counting up what moves are still open."

They tried to think of who might have tipped Luke off because, as they were an illegal outfit, they had their paranoias and, in general, spooled considerable mental energies trying to figure Wentworth.

Luke just had to have a second bowl of chili. Who should come into Papa Juan's? Hans Eagan with two of the secretaries from work. Eagan had on his usual business suit, a silk aloha shirt and dark sunglasses. The ladies were part of the bait that potential clients go for. Wentworth knew immediately what Eagan was up to. Mexican food always led the executive to tequila and tequila led to coke and coke led to bed—today with these two. Luke tried to be beguiling and bought rounds. Eagan savvied Luke's con immediately and thought about beginning an argument. That would make winning the ladies over more difficult. Maybe Luke will talk himself out or get jumped by some foolish ploy. Had Hans seen Luke in self-confident action in the last hours, he would not have placed any chances on the boy burning out his tongue. After an hour and a half of slow eating and drinking it came around to the only point, "Have you girls ever been balled while high out of your minds in a sauna?"

"No, never."

"How'd everyone like to spend the rest of the working day getting off?"

They paid the check and left. Luke went with Amy to her car (hell, he could afford a parking ticket) and Hans took Betty (who had the six foot long racer's body) and folded her into his XKE.

The three boys stuck around the one metal Rabbit of uninteresting color, their fledgling paranoia developing into a four story Cyclops. They deployed themselves at various locations away from the vehicle in case agents were on the way to apprehend them.

After three hours of watching for the dick to return, they decided that they hadn't been turned in and that Wentworth was "on the run." "That's his smartest move." "Should we plant a bomb in the car?" "What? Here, in the open street?" "Leave it to get ticketed and towed." "If he is taking off, he won't be back for it." "A friend might pick up the car after receiving instructions." "The directive's 'no unnecessary corpses'." "Sonofabitch." "We'll get our licks in later."

By now the three were hungry and discussed where to go eat. One of them piped, "There's a Mexican place not far away that serves big margueritas."

Another said, "What should we do about Wentworth?"

The third one replied, "Nothing. If he's around, he'll have to show up if he wants to get any further."

"Right. Let's go."

As it turned out and rapidly made itself apparent, the couples had been cross-matched. Amy feverishly wanted Eagan. Eagan wanted both, but would settle for Betty over the obviously too eager Amy. Betty knew that Hans was not someone that anyone could hold onto, but that Amy was going to try it. Wentworth was too busy telling himself that it was OK to take the day off, even though he hadn't done enough to deserve the good time he was headed for.

Amy was not being particularly friendly on the way up to Eagan's house and she professed, "Honey, I'm sorry but I've lost interest in this sexist little number Eagan's planned. Can I drop you back at your car?"

In all innocence, Luke said, "Leave me at Hans'. I prefer to make my way back from there." Amy continued to act ill until pulling into the ranchero's driveway, then recuperated her health, interests in life, and total enthusiasm in the afore-outlined project.

After a few drinks and a round of the white stuff, normality returned—no one much cared who liked whom, read what, had seen which movies, went to the races, flew a jet, played golf, or overindulged in any excess except the present ones. Mentally and physically stripped, the world is erotically observable and lusciously relaxed. The lie to lie next to is the one that won't knock you to the floor.

XII. IS WENTWORTH
DOOMED?

Wentworth was pretty lucky. Betty liked him almost right away. Her former boyfriend was an Arabian prince who was short in every way and cheated on his promises.

As I said, Betty had formed a fondness for our hero and wanted him to keep on coming around.

He liked her as well. She didn't have the usual graceless mannerisms of a tall woman not completely in control of her frame. He wanted to take her home with him; she wanted to take him home with her. Luke thought about Ed and all the other messes in his place. After awhile, he conceded to try out Bet's.

At about seven o'clock, a cab was called and the two wished Hans and Amy a joyful goodnight. Luke felt bad, leaving his pal in the coils of a viper—just look at what he'd got—but, what can one do when one sees the floodgates of a brief happiness open, but accept the gift, and begin to swim.

The real reason that Luke was so attractive all of a sudden was based on the fact that Better had not quite gotten rid of her undesirable Arabian friend. Bets had seen Wentworth's gun tucked discretely under his sports coat at the time when the festivities were about to begin in rogering earnest.

"A gun," the lithe switch cut. "A gun will scare and keep Ahmed off." Wentworth had thought that he was winning the lassie's affection with his cute, hard-boiled, clear-headed, not overdone, winsome patter.

Betty needed to pick up her car, an older Mercedes sedan, and Luke needed to grab at least a few changes of clothes from either home or office.

They dropped by Luke's office to save driving time. Shirley had been there, cleaned up a little, and had left a note, which came close to sounding as if the woman was threatening to give notice if expected to be a domestic.

The two ladies he had specifically met at Poule's had called asking to share Luke's company at wildly different hours on the day present. Luke regretfully crumpled the note after making sure that he still had their calling cards in his wallet. Judith had not phoned. There was a waiting list of clients on the center of his desk. Luke put a checkmark next to the cases he wanted to accept.

Well, that was that. The sun never sets except again and again on the worried world of business.

The phone rang. It was Ingrid in a frenzy to complain. "Do you know what your daughter has done to me?" was the general tone of the private attack. And "no," he didn't, and "yes," he'd come out and have a talk with her.

"When?" his ex asked.

"How about tomorrow evening?"

"What's wrong with right now? Things are wrong right now!"

"Tomorrow will have to do."

It was obvious to Luke that he'd be needing the car. He got Better to drop him off at the lazy, not yet ticketed thing and then followed behind her up the canyon, where she had a house—one of those things that promised one day to crash down the cliff.

She had not told Wentworth that she kept dogs. He could hear them barking as he drove up behind her. There was a Rolls Royce parked in the garage. That was an unpleasant sight added to an unpleasant sound. Luke began to smell a rotten fish under his shoe. He checked for his can of mace and moved his gun from the shoulder holster to his pocket.

Luke contemplated backing out of the drive and just going over to his ex-wife's to have that talk when he heard voices tangled in argument raised in the guts of the house. A more eager knight would have run to the rescue and dispatched whatever unpleasant dragon's odor might be fouling the air.

Wentworth resented being used (only this time?) and walked leisurely to the front door. He heard strange-tongued and foreign-accented threats being thrown, a nasty rebuttal, and then the sound of a hand slapping a cheek in dog-bark accompaniment. So they were not attack or guard dogs, only onlookers, Luke reflected. He lit a cigarette and listened outside the door to the scuffling for a few drags, until the noise reached a pitch. One of the combatants foreshadowed more barbarian behavior by breaking what sounded like a bottle against a coffee table. Betty's voice, "No!"

Luke put his hand on his gun and confronted the five-foot-three prince, who was going after the girl with a curved dagger. The bottle she'd broken had cut her finger.

Upon perceiving Wentworth. At the thought that Luke might, even possibly, be hired, the prince found rage and turned his anger upon the intruding eye.

In a dumbly dramatic gesture, the prince lifted his blade over his shoulder and made a rush to deposit it in Wentworth's chest. This struck Wentworth as extreme since he had the gun.

Luke had wished afterwards that he had had time to use the mace. He hated the loud noise of a discharge in confined places. It seemed to him that he was always firing the thing. And always in someone's living room.

After having shot the Arab in the foot, the prince collapsed, nearly stabbing himself. Luke went to comfort the chap, offer advice, aid and counsel about treatment and cure, offer sympathy and apology.

The prince shrieked wildly at Luke's attempt to make amends and turned his panicked stare at Betty, who was nodding slyly in the corner of the room with an enormous smile hanging from her face. The prince demanded an ambulance. Betty left for the kitchen to make the call.

Luke was trying to pry the prince's three hundred dollar shoe off his foot (left foot) to wrap up the wound and stop the gushing blood from flowing out over the blue carpet. The prince finally realized that Luke was not enjoying himself and began to stop his threats. Luke was alleviating the pain. Could the wounded party have a drink? "Sure," Luke said and got, "Bourbon?" "Sure. That's fine," from the liquor cabinet.

Betty emerged from the kitchen to report that the ambulance was on the way. So far no police. How to explain the wound to the drivers—no explanations necessary, this was a very private service. She'd used it before and the Arab would be paying his own bill. He'd come at her with what was really only a letter opener from the writing desk.

The dogs were spaniels and had swum back and forth and around the room in a group while the melee lasted. There was one black male and three almond-yellow colored females. The male lay passively in front of a sliding porch window watching— who knows what. One of the females was licking blood from the original place the prince was hit, another tried to lap its tongue over the exposed wound, while the last wanted his face. He pushed them fiercely away and spilled his drink.

Luke asked for some antiseptic and bandages. Better brought them, along with some shears. She unhesitatingly gave Luke the shears. Suppose the prince wanted to poke her with them? Betty retired to the kitchen to ponder Luke's supper and other rewards, but was soon drawn back into the living room by groans and shouts.

Never underestimate the want of bloodlust or revenge inherent in anyone trying to ease the hurt of a humiliation. After treating the wound, Ahmed tried to grab the shears, which had been left so temptingly close by, and jabbed Wentworth in the side, below the fourth vertebrae. Luke reacted. Maced the man. Ahmed howled, tried to stand up on his debilitated foot, and consequently crashed down against a glass coffee table bruising his opposite knee.

Betty came in while Luke was calling Ahmed an oaf. "You now can take care of your own foot and cut the bandages with your incisors." The prince glared at him. Was about to tell Luke that he'd live to see the day when he would see Luke standing up to his neck in camel dip, when they heard a vehicle in the drive.

The police. Some neighbor, probably the technical illustrator who complained when the stereo was turned up too loud, had objected to the shouting. The ambulance pulled up behind the black and white. Ahmed fabricated a story about how Bet had lured him up to the house to rob him of some valuable jewelry. He was outwitnessed and, there was no evidence of loot. Ahmed screamed that they had hidden it while he writhed on the floor, helplessly wounded.

The shorter, older, brighter of the officers took Wentworth aside and got what seemed a more probable story, that the beguiling female was using him as weight to get rid of stale goods. It was obvious that Luke was not at all happy about having been used, thrown to the dogs to make slaughter of, etc. And the policeman knew this as highly believable, especially the part about almost having been stabbed. There were the shears all right and they had ... Hey! Wentworth hadn't noticed before, but a nice slice of coat was missing. Would Luke like to press charges against the lying S.O.B.? No, Wen hated courts. Let him go. Doesn't know who find revenge against yet.

O.K. Haul the citizen to his feet. Away you go. Luke's appeasements came in the forms of wine (excellent wine), a tablet of a powerful drug that relaxed him to death while dinner was being made, a stimulant, a relaxant, excellent food, coffees and sherbets, a massage, on this, on that, and soon all that hypocritical anger was as dissolved as his body. Luke was lead here, over there, expanded, contracted. Elastic Man. The perfect jello with a rod of steel. An egoless oneness sat on him as his soul rolled itself out of the terror of the uncharted surrounding universe and into an amorous sleep. A host of deviant angels sang bawdy hymnals to him in praise his (now flaccid) adventure.

He woke up in the middle of the night, 3:30 or thereabouts, and Bets was gone. He was badly hung over and threw himself into the, ugh!, pink bathroom with orange and purple wallflowers. He made his fingers jerk through the medicine cabinet full of unlabelled bottles, until he found ones that he could assume were reasonably safe. Stamped with a pharmaceutical logo. There was a long hot shower. His motor control was too far away to be call back. Luke sat in the tub while hot lines bounced off his untanned hide.

Wrapping a towel around his middle, Luke stumbled to the kitchen, once over a dog. It didn't want to bite. To the kitchen, where, turning on a stark overhead, he was temporarily blinded. Two tongs of pain sliced through his eyes and lodged in his thalamus. They stung and burned. Just two happy torturers taking their leisure. Get up off your knees, Wentworth. It's only a kitchen light for Crysake.

Coffee was prepared by the shaky hands and eggs were fried without regard for appearance, taste or anything. Faction.

Luke scrounged around for his clothes, which were scattered. A jacket in the front closet, shoes … One shoe was mysteriously under a living room chair. Had a dog dragged it away from its mate? The most curious detail was that his gun had been removed from its holster and slept on the nightstand on Bet's side of the bed. He got a picture of her holding it in the dark after he'd rolled himself over into the mist, and a bit more frighteningly, pointing it at him while he slept.

She was not fun, had not really been fun all day. There was mechanicalness to the way Better did things that revolted Wentworth. The initial attraction faded. Smooth was smooth, but here was a metal that didn't give in at any temperature and Luke thought that he had been hot. It had taken almost fifteen minutes to find the second shoe and it had been located, at last, almost by chance. Wentworth had slumped into the chair it hid under after exhausting his search. He had nudged it with his unshod toe. In touching it, he had first thought it was the prince's shoe still wet with blood. But it was his, slurped over with saliva and mucous.

As Luke made a quarter turn in front of the sliding glass door to go into the bathroom, the rosy-fingered dawn turned half his body a pink crimson. You could see it in the opposite wall's mirror. Went missed it. He stumbled. Forward. Then he backed up, back into Bet's. He'd forgotten something important.

XIII. STRAIGHT BACKING
INTO OTHER THINGS

L uke felt himself left in other than humorous conditions. They were neither comic nor tragic. A chorus of cheery maggots of sang, "Hosanna, get your pants on! There's a fire starting," to the various untwisting fibers of Wenter's inflamed brain.

Wentworth sloppily retired to the kitchen to clear the scuzz off of his shoe. It was time to straighten out his revolting daughter. Jenny warranted excoriation, in the words of mummy, and Luke was ready to deliver them.

Staggering to the car, he spent several minutes finding the ignition (though he had known it well before) and set out block by Incablock to confront his wayward scion. Arriving about five in the morning and blowing the relatively sober horn, he awoke the ex-thing, now woman, to his side. She hauled him out of the drunken auto and into the house in her chartreuse bathrobe.

Wentworth tried to slump onto the kitchen floor, but he righted himself at the snap of a night school karate blow aimed an inch above his groin. Deserved, especially since Luke had been pleading the pretense of a pastoral visit since his removal from the car.

Ingrid started the coffee. It usually brought the oaf around. She wanted to tell him of the frantic phone calls he had been receiving that were interrupting her private life. Luke was not responding. Ingrid conjectured the lout had been overstimulated to exhaustion. She let him pass out.

Ingrid recalled the home movie Luke had of himself playing in a doomed rock band called *Theodore's Phonograph* in an equally doomed early mall. He snapped three strings consecutively on his lead guitar. The other members of the band were disappointed. Luke kept stopping the performance. The tunes had been written by the group's musical wizard. Luke needed only to plug his labored basement competence to show the audience how great they might become. But Luke was better at ping-pong, could defeat even the drummer's lose wristed overhand smash. But here they were, going down in flames. They would never play again. Anyway, not with him in the band.

Luke told Ingrid how he had sulked off to drink some illegally procured blackberry brandy to a corner, alone, rejecting the overtures of two sympathetic young groupies. Ingrid's heart was moved. And later in life, she had seduced the young player. Alas, all too easily.

Here was the dotard sprawled across the top of her elegant dining room table, almost late on the alimony again.

"Throw me into the ocean and let the fish gnaw me awake." Ingrid showed no mercy and unzipped Wentworth's fly. He had never, to his dying fault, been unable, somewhat, to perform.

Luke awoke at about eight a.m. on imitation, mythologically flowered Persian rug of his wife's colonial, wondering how in the *blah* he had ended up there. He jerked himself into the bathroom and took six aspirins. He remembered something unpleasant. What was it? Ingrid had zipped him back up, so there was a lack of evidence.

The bedroom of the wife was next burst into. She greeted him with sour smiles, recriminations and a slow inciting, "OK, lover. Let's have it." Luke tired to explain himself. It was pathetic.

When forced to answer unending questions, he retreated to her bathroom to search for more aspirin. She followed him with her hot forked tongue. More questions. What was up? His daughter was gone.

"What?"

"Gone."

"Gone where?"

"Who knows. She left a letter. It said she was going up North to visit a friend. Tired of living with me! Tired of me!"

"All right. All right. What do you want me to do?"

"Find her, you imbecile. You just can't let her roam around the country getting laid to pay her way along. We're legally responsible for anything that happens to her."

Luke sat on the john and pondered. "I can't leave now. There's a case I have to solve."

"Give it to someone else, you lazy—!"

The great liberation that was Wentworth's the day before ended. Luke watched his ex-wife's hands shake as she ripped open the medicine cabinet and shot her fingers around a bottle of sedatives. The strange admixture of domestic adventuress and adrift mother spiked itself into one of the lobes of Wentworth's brain. We all need alibis to escape these estrous delusions that invade our lives. Our natures are eager to crash out of the daubed high-tension wires fencing them in, but ... Luke pitied his ex while simultaneously sorrowing himself. It was time to try and gently hold, caress, dedicate himself and comfort the creature trembling in shock before him.

The doorbell rang. Wentworth answered. It was his daughter. Before he had a chance to tell her he was glad to see her and have her back, Ingrid rushed past him and grabbed her by the arm, and pulled her into the living room, shouting abuses and smacking the girl in the face. Luke pulled them apart. Mother collapsed into a speechless fit on the couch and Jenny ran to hide in her room.

Luke followed, identified himself at the door and gained admittance. "Why's she? I mean, how long has she been like this?" Luke asked. Out came the tale.

"One of mother's boyfriends wants to marry her and the puke's finally come into enough money to do it. Only, he doesn't want me around. Too wise-mouthed. Too fresh. I hate the asshole/bastard more than the others. He wears dirty underwear and has discolored false teeth that smell of spearmint gum all the time."

O-boy! If he didn't have to pay fucking alimony, he'd be able to do what he wanted. Luke told his daughter to pack. A happy order, apparently. Luke returned to the wife. She had left her post on the couch to make herself something to eat. Fried eggs, I think. The radical change of mood annoyed Wentworth's receptive faculties. "What are you doing in here?"

"I was hungry so I came in here to make something to eat. Do you mind?"

"I'm taking the kid with me."

"Good! I hope you enjoy that mean lip of hers."

"Is it true that you're remarrying?"

"You're going to pay till the end of your days, you dumb-ass dickhead."

Luke piled Jenny's clothes, CDs and assorted accessories into the back of the car. He wanted not to have to throw his friend, Edward, into the sea, but it was equally impossible to consider leaving him around his daughter. He'd come home to table some evening only to find out afterwards that he'd just been served "teenager ala frit."

Luke worried about what kinds of kinky whatnot Ed may be with upon arrival, so he, without explanation, instructed Jenny to wait in the car. He walked forward to brave what might be inside.

Luke walked around the side of the bungalow and peered into the bedroom window. Ed was on his hindquarters going down on one fellow and having it up his bunghole on t'other end. Luke decided to take Jenny out to lunch. There was a passable seafood joint called the Red Snapper only a mile away. He was thinking that he might be able to negotiate Edward's removal over the phone.

Jenny, fortunately, hadn't had food for thirty-six hours. Luke was happy to leave her over a third order of deep fried scallops to go phone.

Edward had the sad news for Luke that he would be leaving almost immediately, within the hour, in fact, aboard a yacht bound for Hawaii. He had just met some "good people." He apologized for the deviate things he'd been doing, but that it was all behind him. He was leaving a check on the kitchen table so that Luke could hire someone to clean up the mess. "Thanks a lot. Goodbye, ol' bud."

"You're welcome. Say hello on the return trip." Luke hoped for a gale as this sentiment passed his lips. Ed's last words were about three guys hanging around that morning. One of them had knocked on the door asking after Luke's whereabouts. Ed said that he'd been rude, shoved the guy off the stoop for not looking normal, ha, ha. He told him to try reaching Luke through his office. There was no description. Just three guys, dressed like hip businessmen, driving a black Continental.

Jenny was going onto a second hot fudge sundae when Luke returned to the red vinyl booth. He noticed all the zits and boils on her face and neck and was tempted to ask her to stop. He let her scoop it down without complaint, lit a cigarette and vigorously pondered his predicament.

It finally made sense to Luke that Dranthus' equation couldn't be as all-important (worth sequestering Poule's Alica for and the ancillary moves with the two dim students) as first believed. Another massively expensive fusion formula, that's all it was. Stuff the university must churn every other day. Things did not add up. It was time to lean on Boil. Boil worked Dranthus' strings.

Luke took Jenny over to the house. She expressed amazement at the mess. Luke started on the kitchen sink, told Jenny to put away her things in the bedroom. She came back a moment later holding her nose and talking through it, "Waaatt kiind offf thinnggg were hew keyping in thare?"

Luke fished under the sink for some spray, tossed it to Jenny, and told her to get back in there. "Holding your nose and make it to the window. Get it open and it'll be OK after a few hours."

"But I'll have to use two hands to get them open. I'll pass out and you'll never be able to save me after I disappear in there." Luke grabbed the can from her and dared the task personally.

XIV. WILL FUSION REACTORS BE AS COMMON AS STEEL MILLS SOME DAY?

Boil thought that it was inevitable. Your yearly energy bill would amount to less than a quarter, even with today's inflation. Wentworth was coming to see him. Boil thought that Wentworth was a chunk of beef unable to appreciate the screen of droplets that rain down, around, and inside one another to make up the common phenomenon called life.

Wentworth was not far beyond understanding electric motors, but when he saw Alica Poule walking across the campus, he flung his visit to Boil's office down with his cigarette and gave chase.

The figure he pursued disappeared through the doors of the Main Library. He glimpsed her form getting into an elevator. Luke ran to see on which floors it was stopping. It stopped on all of them.

Wentworth remembered that Alica's interests wavered between art and science. He went over to a schema of the floor plan and figured she could be on either floor three or six, if she hadn't gone to the bound magazines or special collections.

Alica had gone into the library to use the public facilities located on every other floor. After prettying herself up on the second floor, she bounced down the stairs to meet the date that she had waiting at the bank downtown.

Luke went to the sixth floor first and hurried through the art isles. He bumped his arm against a stack of quatrocento quartos and was all for continuing to glide along when a bespeckled librarian stopped his rush and demanded that he replace the texts.

Luke lifted the red-sweatered bird up and placed her aside. Finding the stairs, he shot down to three and began a like search through the acres of material.

After that, Luke made his way to special collections to give a description of Alica to a grouse old flute who only answered questions with nods and bobs of the head.

The first librarian that Luke turned aside had called campus security. She had been "violated" and starting an investigation of her own.

Luke met no poachers in the bound periodicals and was going towards the entrance when a person (not far away over his right shoulder) welted out the strident phrase, "There he is guard!" but the calm hero, leaning on the nimbleness of his legs, gazed back, and would not offer one look round before flying through the turnstile and glass doors.

Luke ran across campus, back towards Boil's office, not losing the guard until after he'd entered the biology-chemistry building.

Boil had moved from thinking about Raleigh's attempt to colonize Virginia to John Jacob Astor, The Massachusetts Bay Company, Robert Morris (who helped finance the revolution and ended in debtor's prison—ha! Paine didn't think much of him), the Rockefellers, Vanderbilts, Credit Mobilier, Jay Gould, the Morgans and DuPonts before wondering where Wentworth was.

Luke turned into Boil's office a little winded. Al was markedly startled by what might be up. Luke tried to tell Boil. Out of breath and pointing out the door, "I'm being chased. Caught in the act of kicking a soda machine. Broke its logo. Plastic pieces all over the floor. Morons. It stole my dollar."

Boil was pleased to accept that in hopes that Luke would slip and tell more than he wanted to. Little did Boil know how little Luke knew. Boil over-knew almost everything and sized Luke up as a fake connoisseur and brandy drinker when, in fact, Luke was too innocent to be "fake" and only partook of wine and gin.

The conversation was not interesting and I will not report much of it. Boil was a caddy watching a beginning player smash holes in the fairway and the green with his irons. A caddy with a manner pleasing, no matter how wrong the dope got, for the tip.

Luke knew that face. Lying relative, deceitful friend. Luke had been on this case before. They waltzed. Question/answer games first. Boil became aware that he was found out. Luke was not asking for much more than he already had. Luke caught that he was blowing it. Boil's eyes got steadily brighter as he moved Luke's dummies aside. No running. Turn flukes. Get your head the hell out of the toilet!

Boil misplayed a card. False commiseration. Most recently experienced by Luke in his wife's kitchen.

"What's really on your mind, son?"

"I saw Alica Poule last night." Fortunately, Boil did not know where Alica had been. A boiling eyebrow raised itself a few degrees. Al's eye luster dimmed.

"Oh? Where?"

"With your pal, Dranthus," Luke tried. Bad guess. Boil showed he knew he was roasting dead duck again by relaxing.

The sour guard turned the corner just as Luke came out of Aloysius' office. There was no "Hey, you!" yelled at Luke's back. Luke ran from the pounding footsteps. He was left on first as the inning closed.

XV. HOW TO SAFEGUARD YOUR CHILDREN FROM DROWNING

L uke worried about taking Jenny away from her mother. The black Continental appeared in his rear view mirror as he pulled onto the Santa Monica Freeway. Would he be shot at while caught in traffic?

Ed had been accurate enough. This troika was not a plus one version of the pair that had molested his oriental lunch. Much smoother. Looked like they were betting about whether or not Luke was able to snatch an I.D. from his fascinating mirror.

Luke reversed and memorized the plate number. They were speeding up. The next exit wasn't for another two miles. Luke wheeled into the passing lane, stalling their overtake. They dropped back. He could see one of them pointing excitedly back at the exit sign. The driver gestured back, moving his palm gently up and down. Luke wasn't going to get away.

Luke saw the gesture, interpreted it as a killer's demeanor and put his foot to the floor. He darted in and out of the flowing traffic until he had seven cars between them. There was a screech and in his mirror Luke could see a cloud of rubber rising above the cars in back of him.

Luke reflected on what a waste his life had been. They would be on him in seconds. Luke zipped the gun from its tomb and checked his mirrors. They were doing 90 and coming. Luke held his breath and fired. The gunman, in the back seat of the Continental, was just about set, when the left front tire blew. The Continental swerved and went flying, at a 75 degree angle, out on ahead of Luke and sailed, head up and over the embankment, crashing into a concrete pylon and pulling down some high tension wires. They ignited the collapsed metal box and the car exploded in a day-bright lightning flash.

Luke kept on travelling. The traffic kept on moving. It was a few minutes before Luke heard sirens. He had gotten to the exit and was cruising home down the streets of West Los Angeles.

Luke parked in front of a small playground. The kids came off the monkey bars, swings, and jungle gym to look at the man doubled over, puking.

One brave little greed pot tried to grab Luke's wallet. But, in mid-heave, Luke maced him. The gang of seven or eight kids produced a few knives and started forward. Luke pointed his gun back at them from beneath his shoulder blade. They halted.

"He can't hit anyone like that," a bold knife asserted and took a step forward. Luke shot the kid's pinky off and the others scattered.

The bullet had smashed through the knuckle. The punk had his mouth open, unable to scream. Luke was shaking. He went over, picked up the knife, folded it, put it in the kid's pocket. He entwined his fingers in the kid's hair and, pulling the head back, put the gun barrel into the kid's mouth. This shivered the boy into a faint. Luke was content. Time to escape the scene. So far no cops. Luke needed to hide his car and quickly dump the plates. Luke always registered his cars in the names of people recently moved to Forest Lawn and had sets of spares. Packard's trick. Second use. Last time he'd needed it to shake a religious fanatic harassing Wentworth because he'd envisioned Luke as someone possessed of divine grace.

The suit of sweat he was in made him shake. He wanted to proceed cautiously home, drive at twenty miles an hour, but time was against that. Time was against everything. He should be on his way to marinate Boil and, here he was, skulking home after dispatching some probably instantly replaceable muscle. Act. Get to Boil.

A thousand years had passed before Wentworth reached the bungalow. He hurried past his daughter's interrogatives, jerked the new plates from under the kitchen sink (where they were covered with contact paper and taped to the wall), and had them on the car in three minutes. No cops. No cops. Luke would have pushed Jenny onto her knees to pray "no cops" to accompany his frightened pacing up and down in front of the all news radio station, if he believed it could quell the demons screaming for his blood.

Jenny watched for a while, was hushed at every query, and started for the door to take a walk down the beach. Luke demanded she sit and stay where she was. Jenny finally settled for reading a book, one from Luke's old astronomy days with color pics of barium clouds and high altitude release experiments.

Luke anticipated the particle he was listening for and tried not to tense. Didn't want Jenny, who was watching him so very closely from behind the book, to get wise. Daddy never listened to the radio except to hear track results or listen to a basketball game. And then, only when the game wasn't on T.V.

The dot of news. Luke snapped to attention without showing

a sign. The slaughter was being called an accident. Witnesses reported seeing the speeding car blow a tire, almost crash into oncoming traffic, and explode when hitting, etc. Two of the passengers were killed in the crash (a fist into the groin for Luke here!) and a third person, thrown fifty yards from the car on impact of the collision, died on the way to … (A shower of gold dust to equal to Luke's relief). The missing pinky did not make the news. Luke listened for a full hour more.

"What's for supper, Dad?" Jenny inquired the moment the radio was killed. Luke said they were invited to a friend's and told Jenny to put on a dress. Leather belts, Mexican shirts and blue jeans were all she had.

"OK, then. It can't be that formal. Let's go."

"Oh, where to?"

"Surprise."

They went out to the car through the velvet soft twilight being spoken to by the repeated rush forward, in/return, of the crashing surf.

Luke planned to leave Jenny behind Jack Poule's electric fence for awhile. He didn't anticipate any resistance to the idea, except maybe from Jenny who wouldn't like being stockaded.

The drive through the locked gates that opened upon her father's request excited her. Her eyes gave Jenny away. Fantasy land. Living with mother on Petite Center in Atwater was at the ass end of the world compared to this Brentwood estate. The size of the house disappointed her a bit, but the valet was blond and surfer handsome.

Luke left her gazing at the Mezzo-American artifacts. He went into the study to have a session with the telephone-controlled Poule.

In his study, Poule was gazing rapturously over one of his more prized collections when Wen entered. An army of plastic toys from Japanese rice candy boxes were arrayed on the desk top plain before the colossus.

A recognizable piece was a white "Dumbo" with a green fringed collar and melancholically blue circled eyes. This remodeled elephant was the double of the one who had finally managed to fly in the cartoon film. Anxiety oozed from its scale model form.

There were imitation motorcycles with graphically designed amber kickstands, panzers with armed forces markings, all sorts of misconstructed and redesigned motor vehicles—Fords with Chevrolet hoods and Packards with Bentley frames.

These were all the products of a mad Chinese brain, employed by the rice candy firm in Hong Kong. (Features were combined imperfectly, but in exact detail.) Poule was completely aware of the toys' defects, enjoyed them fantastically because he believed them to be "art." Poule needed an approving remark from Luke.

Luke was not quite in the mood for yellow colored BMW's with pink kickstands. Jack believed Luke must be profoundly disturbed. No right-minded person could fail to appreciate … Luke explained that he had definitely seen Poule's daughter that afternoon. He named Boil the likely mastermind of the plot embroiling Alica. He'd electrocuted three men in Jack's service, blown off a finger, and that his daughter required sanctuary.

Jack was so extremely understanding (My, this man's a murderer, killed three people without real provocation and hysterically blown off the digit of an innocent boy), agreeing to take in Jenny and to provide him with a company car. Luke still did not believe that "things were safe." Jack was thinking "Call the police. You've hired a madman to find your daughter. It's a mistake."

Jenny was shown in and introduced by her father. Jack was

secretly revolted by her pimples and proletarian clothing, but sent her to his kitchen to be provided for all the same. What if Wentworth's story was coherent?

Jack unrestrainedly answered questions about Alica between telephone calls. Luke found out very little. Poule was too busy answering the calls of empire to oversee the personal development of people outside his staff.

Intelligence creates many degenerate streets. Luke had known a few. People, outside Luke's range, had sucked, screwed, and loudly wandered outside the range of his perception. His daughter was safe. Poule agreed it was strange that Alica should be moving so freely about.

XVI. IN WHICH WENTWORTH
LEAVES OFF THINKING

Wentworth is beginning to concentrate in on his duties. He left for the loudest bar that he could find. Periods have no single, fixed durations. Luke stumbled into a place inhabited primarily by mostly working stiff nineteen year olds. The band was called "Raven" and not after Poe. They played idiot songs from the late 60's and early 70's, proposing conditions that would never come. Second generation puppets have even less force than first. Especially ridiculous was the old couple, a toothless woman and an unspeaking gray-haired lad. Their daughters would come back to their table to report on how "groovy" the place was between tunes.

Luke retreated after seven incompetent numbers and four beers. He felt sick as he passed dope smokers in the parking lot. Nothing really important ever happened, inside or out. The world. What did it take to understand? Dranthus' formula. Well, he didn't understand that either.

Poule had loaned Luke a white Continental. Luke thought of his victims' charred bones. He was supposed to return it to one of Poule's ladies in the morning and pick up a rental car. Luke dreaded meeting with one of Poule's associates. He needed to remember his fear and pain, and stop playing around. Around Poule, or any of his constituents that seemed impossible.

Young girls in tube tops were attracting Luke's eye. Had his flesh also once been so fresh? "Old " "Weary." Those words hadn't meant anything only a few years ago. He didn't know why, but he went back into the bar. He was missing something. Had to figure out what it was.

Luke had had interesting women. They left him. But, then again, they left everybody. Kept moving on. Luke had once been with a redhead, Linda, before his marriage who had tied him into a knot. She had ended up marrying a Texas millionaire. She had invited Luke to the wedding, trip and expenses paid. Linda had always known that Luke would want her more than any other man, but the body grows old and the mind tires of staying awake. Luke had it with her for the last time at the reception in the attic of the Dallas mansion she was to spend the next sixteen years in, before her older husband died.

Now he got it. The girls he was staring at were here to score hard-working husbands who could keep them at home. Right.

It was a rush for the door, for the warm heat of the cold night.

There's time put in, there's time step out.

Luke put himself back into the seat of the car. On the freeway, back to his place, he mimicked the gesture the assassin had made. Luke despised being that good with a gun. Packard was the one who had encouraged him to go to the municipal range with him and practice. Soon, he was better than anyone on the range. It was a fluke talent in Luke, unrelated to any other. The business of detective needs a lot of training. It requires considerable adroitness to explore places others would drown or could not squeeze to fit into. Luke had served a fairly short apprenticeship with Packard, less than two years.

A thorough detective must understand a lot about other avocations. He must be a little of a henchman, a tincture of the wit, four drains of a confidence man, knowledgeable about some basic electronics (the surveillance end of it was mushrooming to Luke's chagrin—fanatics, those people would bug their mothers), be able to understand accounts, know as much of the law as could be handled (could never know enough there. Lawyers were magicians as far as Luke was concerned. They could reduce a large estate to the worth of a cottage on the Irish coast in a twinkling if necessary), be adept with firearms, explosives and knives, handle assailants, the list might go on, but the point might be this, to a greater degree or less it's pretty much the case as with all other things, you know nothing till you know all.

Luke had been projecting himself onto events pretty much— just as anyone projects when they see someone they want, but are simultaneously afraid of alluring with more effort than a word or a look because a jump into another's existence brings in the gallery of disappointed lives and reeky interests and friends. He leaned back at the wheel of his shiny, white-walled adventure and tried to decide who to maneuver against next. He thought of employing someone he had worked with before to become intimate with Obolus. It wouldn't take much time to get this particular operative close to Oscar. Luke calculated the cost and decided to give this young person a call.

Luke pulled over in front of the taco place (where he had once bitten into a pop-top in his tamale) and gave Randy's number a try. After thirteen rings Randy's mother answered sleepily. "Randy's on a job that won't be quits for three more days. Call back then. Ah, Luke. That you? Want to come over?"

The day mommy and Randy and he had shopped for supplies

at Frederick's of Hollywood appeared in Wentworth's mind. Families with carts filling with black lace underwear, gadgets, hardware, and other devices through the warehouse-sized building drained from Wentworth's mouth a, "No. Too busy tonight. Another time. Soon. Have Randy call me when he's free." Mom was into harnesses, cat-o-nine tails, wet games and leather. Luke was a "normal" man. He returned perturbed to his vehicle because now the awful hurt to be with a woman had whipped a stiletto into him.

Following the rat-turn thoughts through the labyrinth of phosphorescent memories flooding through the opened sluice of the man-boy's brain would not advance the plot a bit. He could not remember the number he needed.

Luke was reliving his first, second, and ninety-ninth times. In haystacks working as a farm hand one summer, on mountainsides, in alleyways—up, down, group, individual, sloppy, sweaty, profound, insipid, nasty, kind. Oh, he wanted some! It was to live for to have some. He even slid back to the days when his birth control method consisted of masturbating twice before coitus, believing the depleted sperm count made it safe for forty-eight hours. On a flight once to Chicago, with a one-armed woman from Waco. On a bus to Tampico with four-eyed twins. He was almost back to the bungalow. He was back. He sat in the front seat awhile letting his recollections flow out with the tide. Inside, he took a shower. After snarfing an omelet he had difficulty preparing (all his sullen nervousness), he slumped off to bed.

It was probably the late meal that kept Luke from sleeping peacefully. There he was a helicopter pilot scurrying over jungle treetops in search of a landing patch. Unending jungle. Full of howling monkeys, toucans and snakes. He could see the snakes, intertwining, kissing, developing human heads, sprouting arms, constructing tables so that there could be such a thing as "tea."

He was out of the mechanical grasshopper. In a passageway that seemed to him vast and incapable of having been constructed by snakekind. It was lit from above by windows that only allowed an attenuated light to pass through their opaque planes. The cool and moist air was sweaty and cold and wrapped around him.

The walls sweated too. Sounds, cries, and hollow moans, the shouts of insults, slaps and a corpse-like odor began to drift to the spot from which Luke refused to move. "This part will be over soon and go away. I'll be somewhere else and be shown more interesting things."

From off in the far distance, torchlights approached. As they came closer it seemed to be a hooded procession of monks, but instead of marching silently forward, they gesticulated frequently and emitted sounds like beasts.

Luke wanted to move away but his feet had become tentacles that had forced themselves through cracks in the floor. He would be subjected to seeing the procession of faces as they passed.

They were all the faces of beautiful women. They looked into his eyes as they passed. Their hands though, were old, eighty-year old hands whose blood vessels were swollen and fingers knotted in arthritis. One woman, a green-eyed redhead, stopped. The others continued to pass. She put a mutilated hand, hanging together with atrophied strands of yellowed muscle, on his shoulder and shook him. "Luke, Wake-up!"

Judith Poule was standing over him with a worried, bitter frown. Luke looked trepidatiously at her hand—she asked condescendingly about what was wrong before realizing that he was returned. Luke expectorated a series of nobby coughs. Pain, panic, and fright. Take away this mask and rush us to the moment of our death. No? Well, then—what do you want? Just keep on livin'. Judith put her hand under Wenter's pillow—propped up his head, assuming he had been drugged and would have difficulty in attending her questions. "Listen, baby. Daddy says you've seen little sister. Is that so?"

"Huh? Huh? Oh, Judith. Your sister. This afternoon on the campus. Yeah."

Judith let Wen's head drop. She callously moved away asking directions to the phone. Luke tried refusing an answer, but saw eyes that were ready to burn him to ash. Luke pointed an index finger to the kitchen. Judith strung the cord out the back door. Even straining his delicate ear, he could not hear. Drowned by the evening wind. Luke expected her return after hearing the tele replaced on the hook. He was preparing a speech, when he heard her gunned engine streak off.

Luke stretched frantic hands for keys, shoes, wallet, accessories, and loose bills on the bureau. Keys? Where were those car keys? On the stoop. The Continental wouldn't start until he's reconnected the distributor. What time? No watch. Too late to to try and follow. He trudged back into the house.

He got one shoe off when the phone rang. He let it drop and limped over to get the call. Poule, wanting to know if he'd seen his daughter. "Which one?" "Did I hire a wise-mouth? Your kids' is darling. Judith." "She just left." Luke retold the story. Drop-in, pull the plugs out, and depart. Poule made grunting, growling noises into the receiver while he listened. Jack was dissatisfied with Wenner's performance. A knock at the door. Would Jack like to hold for a moment? Who was it?

"The police."

"Never mind." Poule hung up.

Luke gritted his teeth as he prepared to answer inglorious questions galore.

Just a few questions here, Mr. Wentworth. Is that right? Yes, yes. Did you know Mrs. Foster very well? The neighbor? Well, no. I mean I saw her around once in awhile, but never socialized beyond borrowing a pinch of tarragon for a stew one night. Hadn't he been reading the papers? Never read the papers. Mrs. Foster had embezzled over $35,000 from the savings and loan she'd worked at and turned up dead this afternoon in the trunk of an abandoned Buick without a dime on her. Did Wentworth know the names of any of the divorced woman's gentlemen friends? As far as Luke had observed from looking out his window one full moon's night about three years ago after he'd just moved in here, Mrs. Foster was a lesbian, or at least bi-sexual. She and a friend were, you know, spooning in the tidewater, having a two hour cats yelling on-the-back-fence time of it. It happened regularly about once a month, but Luke hadn't seen the woman or been around his own place in that long. They should get in touch with his ex-boarder. He'd had her over one night, picked her up along with a friend at the local bar about two weeks ago. And where was the friend now? On a yacht bound for Hawaii, a day out. Radio on board? Dunno. Name of the boat? "The Occasional Core." Funny name for a boat. Yeah, funny name. Anything else you can tell us? Yeah, one of her girlfriend's names, a steady girlfriend is Alica Poule. How do you spell that, Pool? P-O-U-L-E. Well, thanks. Goodnight. You're welcome, officers, good luck.

Emmy Foster snags $35,000 and ends up in a trunk. "Woooweee!" Luke was on his way to the toilet when the phone rang again. He hated holding it for too long. And it, through the exchange with the cops, was beginning to ache. It was Poule calling back to find out how much trouble he was in. Luke had difficulty persuading him the visit was unrelated to any of their affairs. "Read about it in the paper. A woman stole $95,000 from a savings and loan. She happened to be my neighbor. She wound up in a trunk without a penny on her and one of the last people to see her alive is a flako who was staying with her and who's on his way to Hawaii aboard a private yacht called "The Como No." Luke's loquaciousness again won Poule's confidence.

He was on his way back to the toilet with a violent ache in his crotch when the phone rang again. It was Jenny, calling to complain about her confinement. "You'll stay there and like it till this thing's over!"

"What thing?"

"Let it be a mystery to you," Luke painfully uttered and hung up. The phone rang again, but Luke figured it was Jenny calling back. He walked to the phone with murderous intent, verified the voice, and allowed the voice to crake as he stalked off. "Well, sell me a polyester life!" Luke yelled as he poured out his relief.

XVII. IN WHICH LUKE FINDS HIMSELF

L uke came back into the kitchen, replaced the dead phone and started some water for coffee. He mulled over the night's visitors and calls whilst twirling a cup around his index finger. A car was pulling up. Things might be …, so Luke fetched his gun from the bedroom. As he was picking it up, he heard the screen door snap.

It was the tall and trim Better, dressed in silky white and swinging a matching pocketbook around. Repugnant feelings drove around Luke's little track waving flabby hands and throwing rubber kisses out the rolled down window.

"Making coffee? Can I have some?" the Bet began. "Sure." As he walked by her through the door, he avoided a leg raised to trip him and grabbed her foot. "Hey, let go!" "Firm." Wentworth let go, ducking the purse as it whizzed by his ear.

He couldn't hit her, but grabbed her by the shoulder and started to force her to door. "No time for glazed secretaries tonight. Stop back when you're straight."

"Get me some coffee. He came back, madder than a bear and bruised me up." She lifted her longish dress to reveal purple scars. "Why couldn't you have taken care of him more thoroughly?" Here she wriggled out of Luke's hold, sat down at the kitchen table and did a little crying—cursing what had been and still needed to be done. "I want you to take the creep out of my life permanently." She reached into her pocketbook for a gorgeous wad of hundreds and fifties.

It occurred to Wentworth that the reason his gun had been on Bet's nightstand was for protection and not decadent amusement. Ahmed could have come vengefully snarling out of the hospital at any time. Finally, she'd become so anxious about the possibility, she just left. Ah, some motivation, explication. Luke was singularly sympathetic for an instant. He stared at the delicious woman happily until, in uncontrolled vehemence her face crashed, became a frown. She glared up at Luke demanding an answer to her proposition.

Luke proposed alternative actions in an attempt to calm her, but she screamed, "You dense bastard! Don't you understand! I want the sonofabitch dead!"

Luke felt embarrassed for having tried to put her in soft focus. "OK. Where is he?"

"Back at my place thinking he's Joe Hercules."

Luke slid by the table, scooped off the money, went into the bedroom and donned his gear. She ran in after him, giving instructions about where to do it, how she'd like it done and the like. "What shall I do with the corpse?" Luke asked. "Aren't you afraid the police will remember very clearly and precisely where it was that they had to deal with this clown—shot in the foot at your place, found a little later dead? Don't you think they'll be tracing him back to you?"

Luke, your logics are going to overwhelm us! Betty put a finger to her mouth. "Give me back my money!" Luke rolled it out of his trousers. She made a grab for it. He pulled his hand back. She glowered. He handed it to her peaceably.

"What do I do now?" Before Luke could answer, she'd spied the bed and, looking around, stared at the furniture and corners of the room. "Sure smells funny in here." She proceeded to remove her dress and slide away under the covers. "Bring me my purse before you climb in after."

Luke glided into the kitchen, plucked the purse, locked the door, slammed off the light and returned to his slithering, divaricate diva. "Oh, and a glass of water." About face. Edison called back. Turn of the willing wrists. Splosh, splash. Thomas condemned. The slow funeral march return.

"This is not worth it," Luke noted, telling himself as he watched her swallow a few ampoules, head back. She looked up, smiled and invited the shy boy in the birthday suit in.

Writhing around, things became familiar. And, after half an hour, dynastic. There was gunpowder to get things going. He tried to mow her down. She was coy. He had to reinvest. The paints, finishes, dyes, pigments, heavy chemicals, acids, cellulose plastics, rayon and cellophane era. Next there was basic research, internal development (Luke had almost found himself!). Synthetic rubber and nylon, a study of her molecular structure got him through another hour. Then, at last, into the billions! Consolidation of operations and strong marketing programs had Bets moaning in more ecstasy than she had known in a week. Olla! The honeycomb was filled and the drone dropped exhausted. What could be the future hold after such an Olympian triumph! Luke rolled over into a sleep transcending those experienced by now long-deceased padishahs.

She got up. After pacing around awhile, returned to bed, and consented to stay by his side. Noises. A pair of flies taking short hops across the room, the refrigerator jumping on, a mill wheel turning the green diseased pond of her brain. It kept her awake for what seemed hours, but was less than twenty minutes. Her last desire was to be up and out of there in the morning before the "over-reasoning snot" woke expecting her to be "nice."

Wentworth was being caressed by the soft divine will of God until eleven in the morning. He got up feeling refreshed and glad to see the package of sickness had picked itself up and gone.

Nearly lunch time. What a wondrous day! Luke examined a pimple about to erupt. The phone stopped him from prying out the last tiny nipple of pus still hiding under the surface of his flesh.

Who? Who? Would you like to subscribe to a new and exclusive magazine devoted to increasing the awareness of already select individuals? A complete and unlimited world of sensual pleasure comes to your very door! Luke asked for a sample copy to be sent, but the voice informed him that an issue would come out as soon as the subscriber list was built. "What? Not enough steam up for a real launch?" Luke nastily asked. The offended contralto rang off. Wentworth snickered. On a shitlist again. Who had sold him this time? *Playboy*, *Fortune*, *The National Observer*, *Bank of America*? Bah! What did he care. It was better than being molested by insurance salespeople. They left danger dancers alone.

XVIII. IN WHICH THE GENERAL GELATIN DOESN'T MASTER MATTERS

Luke hardly knew why he was so exuberant. After the calls, fatally disheartening dreams and visits of last night, how could he now be so exultant? "It must be the high point of my bio-rhythmic cycle," Luke thought, hardly remembering how much effort had made to stud him into this euphoria.

He went Japanese—with oyster soup, cucumber scallion salad, sushi, shrimp tempura and batter-fried vegetables. After six rounds of saké he was "confident" that he would have Alica Poule in his hands inside of two more days. Luke had to be fairly drunk to forget that he'd been marked for execution. With the particular organization that was after him, it took longer than usual to replace killers.

The idea? To get Alica and be free of the chasedown. The next big deal would come along (after the business that she was needed for either succeeded or failed) and he would be forgotten about.

As he came out of the restaurant, he began to see that it might be otherwise. The saké mixed with the glaring L.A. sun made the end of this case seem much further away. "Far away, far away," the tune began to repeat in Wentworth's head, "and she wore it for her lover who was far, far away." Luke put a hand on his stomach. Getting round. Baby, that's not good. You don't want to be a fat detective. Back to running two miles on the beach every morning. Yeah. As soon as this job's over.

The 30,000 fibers in Wentworth's auditory nerve assembled a different tune as he bent over, trying to fumble the keys to the Continental. "Mr. Wentworth?" The voice, behind him. Luke's neck hairs stiffened and muscles pulled spasmodically. Turning, he could see that he was being addressed by an unknown quantity. A kid in his mid-twenties, looking three degrees less manufactured than Frankie Avalon. A messenger. No bulge under the arm, but maybe he knew enough karate to make dog food out of Wentworth.

"I'm a friend of Alica Poule's. My name is Robert Iosue. She's asked me to talk to you about last night."

"How do you spell that?"

"Spell what?"

"Ja-sa-way."

"What? Are you here, Mr. Wentworth?"

"It's an Italian name, isn't it?"

"I-O-S-U-E, a hundred miles northeast of Rome. All right? Can we go somewhere more private?"

"I like it fine here," Luke said getting his hand around the vial of mace in his pocket while pretending to fish for a cigarette. Robert offered one of his. Wentworth accepted it. "OK. Let's go somewhere." Bobby looked towards the front of the Japanese restaurant. "Aw, not in there. They have lousy coffee and my gut's not ready for of green tea. I need to sharpen my picture.

Let's walk a block to the greasy spoon." Bob eased. Luke could see visions of raw fish wriggling through the conservative brain. Luke liked the kid. The teaser about "last night's events" had been well-handled. Not so heavy it tried to knock you down, and not so light it didn't get your attention.

The conversation engaged in while turning the block was one in which the investigator tried to find out all he could about Jack's cute family. Iosue hopped around avoiding direct answers. Apparently he had something very specific to impart and that was it. A quiddity that refused to be penetrated before ready. Wentworth held open the door to "Emmy's" for Bobby. Luke excused himself before the hostess podium. "Go ahead and find a booth. Order me three cups of coffee."

"All at once?"

"All at once."

Luke returned cheerful and slid in across from Robert. Bob was faced toward the window and did not move. Wentworth got up and kept on walking. Out the door, fast. Bob's eyes had been open, but staring at the mother tomb.

Wentworth rushed back to his car, approaching the parking lot cautiously, watching for signs of humble friends too shy to show themselves immediately. His Banlon shirt was filthy with sweat. He saw one guy strolling around the entrance to the Japanese restaurant. Wentworth turned flukes and sought a bus. Time to go public.

Luke got on a bus headed for Maywood (he was up near the civic center) and rode it to the end of the line. Staring at a boy reading space, cowboy, and war comic books (he had a stack with him), Luke tried to figure out who his enemies were and how many this time. Bobby Iosue was "oozing light" partially because of the W's careless manner.

Luke spent the next few hours riding different buses that

would get him across town, close enough to Brentwood so Poule's haven could be reached "reasonably" by taxi. He got as close as West Hollywood. By around six o'clock, exhausted and struggling, he asked himself why he hadn't quit for a few weeks before this job started and taken a Mexican vacation. "Greed" was the answer to his question. But Luke settled for telling himself it was "need." The alimony payment was falling due.

Luke went into a topless go-go bar and drank a few while the bartender made his cab call. The breasts were all silicone. At least now the shifts in matter were kinder. Remember inserts and those tell-all scars? Luke left to stand on the street to wait for the cab. The mushy heat was preferable to the air-conditioned nightmare. A miller belongs in a mill. Your private eye … Luke's mind kept stopping these clichés from completing.

A black dog with a red ribbon was hunting its way toward Wentworth from down the street. He was ready to step his catself back into the bar when he saw his cab struggling to pass a fat Buick driven by a slumped over octogenarian. Estimating the arrival times of the approaching parties, (the dog was stopping to sniff inside storefronts, a heavily shoed foot extended itself from one edge, driving the hound on). Luke deduced he could stay on the street and got into the back seat of the cab just as the dog began a snarling run at his disappearing leg.

Iosue's eyes (staring ahead at the orange cushion across from him as the blood gathered inside the shirt to form a pool beside him) travelled the top of Luke's skull. Projection. A magic lantern show. One candle. No more birthdays for sad-dead Bobby.

Luke had himself dropped seven blocks from Poule's gate and walked. Wentworth's cautions were forming a phalanx. He made himself known over the electronic call box. He asked for a car to pick him up. A few minutes later, the valet showed behind the wheel of his Rabbit. Luke imagined slides of Jenny and the valet. Luke gave the driver his Svengali stare. Nothing there. The boy told Wentworth that Mr. Poule was holding counsel with his staff. A place had been set for him, and he was to go in. Luke told Sam (Sam's his name now) to have six double gin and tonics brought to the table as soon as possible. Luke's self-confidence was eroding and we can even tell you that he'd made it to being scared. The cynicism seems to have been bled out of him by the harsh sun of recent events.

Wentworth plopped himself between the old lady and the black woman. The team colors today were orange or green. The black woman was tastefully in green, the matron in orange. Poule, wanting to hold all the wires, tried to embarrass Luke by putting the sword of social grace to Wen's neck.

"Why so rude, Wentworth?" Luke stared up from his drink, retained his "blind to the wall" eye, and announced blandly that, "Someone else. Someone with a message from your daughter got himself murdered this afternoon before I had a chance to find anything out. I had to watch the corpse bleed for just long enough to hate the human condition." Luke, cocking his head, put his eyes on Poule. "You don't mind if I try to extinguish myself a little do you?"

Poule became apologetic and even offered Luke the best of his wine. Luke declined. "It's a gin run to oblivion night. Let them know to keep it coming and I'll be all right. I'm sure your daughter is still alive."

Poule whitened, gave the instructions to keep feeding Luke the booze (in more and more diluted doses). He had to be in shape to go back out there. Poule returned to business. At first, cautiously, but soon with the usual addicted vigor.

The ladies were leaving Luke alone. He stared at all of them for short whiles and long, trying to get them to think he was a desirin' them. He stared longest at the matron who nervously kept on nodding and baring her false teeth to Luke. He kept on marveling at the great grand job some dentist had done. Somehow they didn't make up for the crooked, decayed, yellow, stained, missing and real thing. What would his choppers feel like capped? The lawyers across town were all investing in worry free, quick installation, no-bother teeth these days. It was the latest thing after plastic surgery.

After staring for awhile, he got the compulsion to touch them, to feel how firmly they were held in place. Thumb and forefinger travelled patronizingly mouthward.

"Would you mind if I…?" He clasped the specimen. They came right out, just as he had suspected they would! Alice went screaming from the table causing a considerable stir. Luke regarded the set from every angle that he could think of, including down between his legs. After about three minutes of this, and having twenty-six? No. Alice left. Twenty four, minus one for the glass eye. Twenty three eyes on him, Poule asked Luke if he wouldn't mind putting the pearlies down. Wentworth began to tell the tale of how the other day the fat lady had…, but the reception was bad so he axed the act. The teeth were picked up and conversation resumed.

Cherries jubilee ended the meal along with coffee. Luke hogged a pot to himself. He was the first to try to leave the table, but he was stopped by a vicious cramp that made him speechless. He gesticulated like the madman. They all thought he was anyway. "What now?" Poule asked. Luke could hardly even point out the problem much less articulate it. He collapsed onto his chair. Alice came back. He was glad to see her. "Vicious cramp. Kicked in the knee playing rugby." (What a liar Luke is! It was only soccer.)

Judy, the black woman, took pity on poor Punch and led him away from this impure stage to his room. She folded down the sheets and tucked him tenderly in saying, "Goodnight, Fool," before she turned off the lights.

Shall we descend with Wenthworth into his dreams again or look around the house? Maybe check the whole town to see what else is happening? Let's get away from Luke. He's only going to have alchie psychodramas about what to say to people if they ask him about the corpse in booth ten just now.

Dranthus is someone we haven't seen for a good long while now. He's talking on the phone to a constituent in Zurich about the error in the fusion formula that he had thought he'd found. "I'm still confident that I'm only another three weeks away from really getting it." The listener is bored by now. He's looking out his chateau window at a meteor shower thinking what an insignificant gram of time a human life consists of. He's lost his ego to his work and painfully admires Dranthus' crudity. Edgar can't stop. "I'm going to electrocute all the old methods in one macrocosmic step, Anton!"

Eagan is thinking about tying the girl he's with (someone none of us has met) to her bed and leaving her there to get hungry. She's definitely all for some bondage, but doesn't see the twist Hans is determined to inject into the scenario. Avenue of careless night.

Boil feels bondaged. Alica is talking to him in rapid fire voice from the kitchen where she's fixing him a late night snack, Hunter's buns. She's interrupted the flow of her patter to ask a culinary question. "Al, is there any condensed milk? There isn't? Oh, well, I'll use a substitute." The word flow stops as Alica goes to the fridge for some skim milk.

Boil is turning Alica's attempt at betrayal around in his showroom. He knows that she must be worried about what happened to her messenger friend. Is there anything poisonous in that kitchen? No. Relax. She's trying to overcompensate for the insecurity of her position. He'd like to try the position she told him about last week, tonight. He thinks he's ready for it. Get it while it's still available.

"That's all I can see," says the kerchiefed tent-show gypsy.

"I want to hear more!" says the future general.

I would like "more," too.

Judith Poule is in South Africa to discuss an investment for her father. She is at a party where a few pests are beginning to dismiss their wives and maneuver close to her. Her choice has been preplanned, but there must appear to be a hunt, a trackdown, a struggle, a triumph, a victory. Otherwise, I'm sure that whatever deal's made, the Poules would be getting three percent less than what they have eventually planned to come out with. Sometimes this method doesn't work and then four others get squeezed all the harder. Alica is supposed to be in South Africa. Luke was supposed to have found her. It doesn't matter in this instance anymore, but Daddy still wants her back. While she's been stray an even more clever use for her has appeared in Jack's mind. The operation needs both sisters.

Obolus is at home surrounded by his collection of cats. His new lover has left and he's decided to finish the chapter in the book he's been working on. It traces the development of corporations from carte-blanche land-grant handouts given by the queen (sixteenth century here) to a few of her impoverished nobles to its present form, the giant conglomerate, privately owned and piratically managed, oligarchical machine. It's not a bad book. There are things missing—left out on purpose so that a point or two looks illegitimate. The fun starts when they attack you for it, and you're more than ready to attack back. One of the cats, a Siamese, has jumped up onto the desk. It's seen a moth to stick its claw into flutter around Oscar's light. He's in the middle of a sentence leading to the very most exciting part. The cat receives a quick and callous shove back onto the Persian carpet. Obolus has lost what he was going to say. The perfect phrase had been in his mind! Upset the cat-god. Make sacrifices. Oscar gives up his mission, goes to fill the water bowls and hand out Little Friskies on top of some matutabi, a drug that felines prefer above catnip. Obolus fishes in special places to get it. Oscar recognized a truth. Watching his pets stretched out in ecstasy before him on the floor, he could see its wrinkled abusive face. *It was all stimulation—the act of, the manipulation, the enjoyment* ... He could finish his sentence. The cat-god was kind. Oscar's place was messy. Tie tongues stuck out of drawers as he hurried to explain the use of costumes, funerals, and the universally soft whip in the progress of the rising social, political, and economic tide.

Jenny was out in the yard trying to find Sam. He'd had enough of her and had slipped into town. Jenny wandered the garden for awhile then unclothed and swam, otter-like, in the kidney shaped pool. Lassitude had infected her feelings. Otter strokes and seal dives. Jenny was hoping to be accepted by the philosophy department of an Eastern college. Unlike her parents, she felt she aspired. The phenomenological universe always bathed/embraced her kindly whenever Jenny wanted.

One of Poule's ladies, who had already earned her degree in philosophy from an Eastern college, watched Jenny paddling around in the soup and now extended a hand to help the klutzy beaver out. The friendly exchange of touch led to a meaningful kiss.

Dranthus had hung up the phone, dissatisfied with his friend. The Lilliputians must be made to understand! At this point, Edgar went to his bathroom mirror to wonder how he would look with a moustache. He called Fredericka on to help him draw various shaped and sized ones. At last, he looked like Errol Flynn. There was nothing for it. They simply must have it off with clothes on in the shower.

Boil was smoking a cigarette in bed cynically counting the steps to the old age home. The branchless night coiled around him. The faucet dripped in the adjoining bathroom. Alica had wanted to brush her teeth before sleep took her. The drips drowned Aloysius's meditation. He got up to silence it. Boil ended up in front of the tropical fish tank drinking screwdrivers.

Aloysius fought off giving in to even sadder thoughts and went for a book. The fingers glided over the titles beginning with "M" and worked backwards. Boil settled on a biography of Pedro Alvarado. Cortez Had left Pedro to protect company interests in Tenochtitlan while Cortez marched back to the coast to fight or incorporate a rival expedition that had landed to take over. Pedro gave it all back to the Aztecs. One afternoon he marched his band into a central Mexican square and butchered the people engaged in a mescaline inspired religious ceremonial dance. When Cortez came back he had to fight for control all over again. And the gold? All the gold the Spaniards had first gathered into their possession had disappeared. Where was the gold in Boil's fight? He sighed a sadness that could not be measured. Life always fools you into believing that you have more than you've got.

XIX. TEMPERANCE, SILENCE, ORDER, RESOLUTION, FRUGALITY, INDUSTRY, SINCERITY, JUSTICE, MODERATION, CLEANLINESS, TRANQUILITY, AND CHASTITY

In the morning Luke got up and started screaming. "I want drink, food, and women right away!" Poule sent an emissary to ask Luke when he would be needing a car to get back to the case. Luke informed the flunky that, "Jack's an ass if he thinks that I'm going to leave this room before regaining my nerve."

To regain his nerve and again mount the hunt he, Luke, would have to sweat, stink and immerse himself into such a state of misery, despair and oblivion that he would be happy to return to the streets to find the unidentified dork intent upon murdering him.

Luke wavered, shrinkingly between volcanic torpor and drunken nausea for three days. Plots revolved in his head that all led up to his becoming a totalized nothing. A colony of deaths passed in review. Three quarters of the time, a grinning half-wit stared down at his open-eyed corpse being dissected on the city morgue's autopsy slab.

Who knows what will walk out of the soul of a man. It's an "ummmm" and an "ahhh" and a forest of "ooophs!"

Luke refused to shower or bathe, allow the trays of dirty dishes to be removed, the sheets on the bed changed, the burned out light bulb to be replaced, the woman that they had thrown in to him to leave. About the only thing Luke continued to do was go to the bathroom. It had a bath and shower and one morning he caught the woman trying to use it. She screamed and was rescued.

Soon after they took her away, only half a day more, and Luke came out. He was dressed only in his yellow polo shirt. He didn't bother to pull it down for modesty and walked around the house telling servants to get this and that ready for him. He walked out of the house and threw himself into the pool, staying under for as long as he could hold his breath and awhile longer.

Luke lifted what was left of the crown atop his spinal column above water. The eyelids were closed with the inner membrane painted a tone softer than a flaming light-orange red. The old patched fences, ditches with their weedy edges, fields of outcrop huge grey glacial flowers, spots of color and girls walking around the main street of the town tugging down their cut-off shorts, assuredly, to experience the ecstasy of their own alive skin. Wentworth was seventeen for a roaming moment again. A voice broke the spell. Poule's. "I've just finished playing a champion set of tennis and I feel generous."

Luke couldn't think of Jack as champion of anything beyond bedwetting. He shaded his eyes before opening them. "How long will it take to get a silencer for my gun or a silencer with a gun?"

Jack should have been taken aback. In fact, the question made him deliriously happy. "About a day. Maybe by this evening."

"A thirty eight or larger if you have to get the gun too."

Poule wanted to reply with a clever affirmative, but Luke had turned over twice and was now bobbing through the water.

It is useless not to seek, not to want. When you cease to seek you awkwardly and embarrassingly start to find. Wentworth had boozed, ate, and screwed away what he wanted not to know. And, still, it was there when he talked to himself, when he sweat, when he ached, when he howled for some service of appetite. When you cease to want, then life begins to shove sour stew down your gullet. Oh, to hunger, thirst, and lust everyday afresh! Luke has stopped bobbing and is now in the kitchen at the refrigerator. A maid, older, overweight and almost with a visible moustache, comes in and begins to chide Wentworth. She overlooks near nakedness but not thievery. He slams the avocado colored cooler door shut, puts on his most ferocious face and walks towards the aproned matron. This doesn't seem to do the trick. She's searching the vicinity for an object to assault Luke with. Luke passes by the table, picks up a mallet and tosses it to her and picks up a butcher knife for himself. She decides he's bluffing and stands her ground.

"To the death then!" Luke rushes at her wailing the Beserker breakdown. The maid throws the mallet, which Luke catches on the thigh, but in half a second more he has her in an armlock with the knife at her throat. "Now see what ye done. You've made me want to kill you!" The maid faints. Luke gallantly lets her ample carcass to melt out of his arms.

The screaming has aroused the overalled gardener and he appears, shears in hand. He's always had a craving for the maid.

He knows she saves her every penny. Luke can detect heroics massing in the brutal head. Watch those hedge clippers! Through the other door comes Sam to bring Wentworth the gun and silencer he's requested. He doesn't bother to size up the lump on the floor or the hedge clippers dominating the door. He hands Luke the piece.

"Will this do?"

"Sure." Before Luke can look up, the gardener has gone. "Are they married or something?"

"No. You'd better get your pants on. Judith wants to talk to you up in her room."

"Been screwing my daughter?"

Sam looked shyly at the pattern of the floor tiles.

"Good." As Wentworth walked off, he stepped gingerly over the folded form of the fallen woman. Luke was beginning to see what a common and ordinary thing it was among men to realize, foresee, understand, and predict another's fortunes and what an impossibility it is to do work on one's own.

XX. THE DELIGHTFUL VOID
AND MOANING NIGHT

Luke disregarded the suggestion about trousers and presented himself before Ms. Poule in a wet shirt and unshaven face. Judith herself had on only a pair of tight white satin underwear, fondling herself in a full length mirror when he came in. Luke looked like a big, sloppy dog. She was from a fashion magazine ad. "Don't bother me now. Just sit down." She labored before the mirror for another ten minutes ere she was satisfied.

"You've impregnated my maid." She turned away from the mirror to look directly at him. Luke could have chosen the bed to lie prone and watch from, but he flopped into a wide rattan chair over which hung a discarded chemise and pink, yellow and orange nightgowns. "What are you going to do about it? What compensation can you offer?"

Luke got up and walked towards the door. No words stopped him, but a trilling laugh followed him partway down the stairs.

Luke made for his room and called for shaving articles and clothing. He went into the shower and wove himself out existence. The sound of footsteps brought him back. After drying off, he scanned the growth in the mirror. It was partial disguise enough from a distance. In a few days he would cut it back to sideburns and a moustache and maybe shave the pate. That was a good idea now, and he did it. Wentworth The Unrecognizable. Poule entered and saw the strange face in the bathroom and slipped back out to call the security guard. By the time he arrived, Luke had left his quarters. A general alarm sounded.

Luke walked in on Poule in the library where he was anxiously consulting with his staff about the trespasser. People, ladies and gentlemen, all rushed at Wentworth upon command. They retreated when Luke displayed the gun. The security guard had his out by the time the throng had parted and was going for a shot. It whipped past Wentworth's side, nicking open the skin. Luke, not wanting to stop his own progress, dauntlessly zipped two silent "ffftt,ffftt" slugs into the sluggish ex-army captain's arm. Jack stooped to pick up his fallen weapon. Visions of lost empire boiled in his brain pan.

"Hey, Jack!"

Say, wasn't that a familiar tone?

"You don't want to join those burning up down there yet, do you? I'm no expert at trick shots. How you're slumped over right now, I have no place to hit you except where it's fatal."

"Wentworth? Wentworth? Wentworth you scared me to death."

"Call a doctor. Do you have any cash around here? I need about two thousand dollars."

Poule didn't remain grateful for his life for long. The request for funds put him back into his old harness. He told everyone to leave them alone. The wounded man was howling fiercely and some threats of revenge against both Poule and Wentworth audibly passed his clenched teeth. After being escorted out,

Poule gave instructions for the guard's dismissal and the employment of someone, "Younger and faster."

"Now, what do you need this money for?"

Luke explained his plan about getting Arthur close to Oscar Obolus for purposes of blackmail.

"Arthur's expensive."

"Arthur is quick and cheap, Stingy."

Poule had a wall safe behind a painting done by Moreau on the far wall. The painting was in a weak frame and badly lighted.

"Turn your back." In forty-five seconds out came the cash in very untraceable twenties and tens. "How long before we get some information?"

"About a week. At most."

Jack reminded Luke that his two hundred dollars a day days were over. But in view of the fact that so many unforeseen circumstances had arisen, and the case had become quite dangerous, Luke would continue on at that salary until Alica was safely returned.

"Found."

This last declaration perturbed Poule. He puzzled out what it meant. Luke about-faced and left Poule to suffer, which was what Wentworth wanted.

Arthur, as I remember, was completely unavailable and Wentworth seems to have bluffed Poule out of two grand.

Luke got into the waiting car, a splashy, gray glitter painted Ford, and drove down the drive accompanied on either side by the excited pack of dogs. Luke pulled the mirror onto himself and laughed as slyly and smugly as the devil.

XXI. IN WHICH TWO THOUSAND DOLLARS IS SPENT

If we begin with the inward world of thought and feeling, the whirlpool is rapid and the flame eager and devouring. (Two grand!) That clear, perpetual outline of face and limb is but an image, (Two grand!!) a design in the web, (two, two, two, two, much! Yes! Poker. Poke!) isn't it? Luke usually didn't listen to the car radio. He turned it on. A sermon against sloth and pride was being delivered. He snapped it off.

A car had been stationed outside Poule's gate, a day and night watch. Had they recognized him? They weren't following. But they might have called ahead. Luke chose a destination exactly opposite what the case would dictate. It was about two o'clock and Luke was very hungry. He thought he saw what might be a car following and pulled into a drive-in with a drive-through pick-up window. It was torture to choose an item from the menu. The other car was pulled up, two behind. Luke ordered what he thought would be a normal sized thing, two double-ughs fries and a shake. He parked. The other car parked an observable distance away. Luke turned on a muzak station and tried to keep contented as he munched towards indigestion. This stuff was actually worse than what he got at his ex-wife's. There, at least, he could excuse himself after dinner and go to the john, where he either peed, or pretended to pee by pouring water from a Dixie cup in a stream into the bowl while he took a few of the anti-acid pills he carried when invited to his former home. What a protozoic feeding zone this was! Luke remained placid. Maybe this would make the hawks go away and find some other sparrow to bring to ground.

After consuming his meal, Luke pulled out past the tail. He pretended disinterest and didn't even give his rear view mirror a shot. This doom to doom series of events upset Wentworth beyond toleration. He had to know if these guys were onto him. His dodge was to stop at a downtown hotel and pretend to register. He got into the elevator, pressed second floor and seventh, and got off at two. They wouldn't be able to reach the lobby until the thing was past two and he could come behind and around.

The car that Luke fancied was following him never was. It happened to be going his way by chance. It was a crummy dodge and probably wouldn't have worked anyway. They would have gone to the desk and found Wentworth out. Too cheap to take the room. His mindless oversight struck Luke as he was driving away. Luke attributed his lack of acumen to the days of dissipation. He needed to reforge his nerves with an arresting amusement. The mobile was pointed towards the racetrack.

The appetites of the flesh, the craving for money and the melancholy of passion merged in one Wentworth when he beheld himself in one of the track's pungent bathrooms. Luke blew lunch. His own aroma became unpleasant. Breath freshener and chewing gum failed to completely hide the odor.

Luke deposited himself at the bar and began pounding Patrón tequila and Bohemia chasers. He placed his bets in a stupor and received his winnings in a daze. Five hundred dollars ahead. He began to worry about being rolled. Hallucination. Luke has a nice ranch but the bulls there feed on purple grass while waiting the chance to slice up Luke with their laser eyes.

Wentworth realized he was close to passing out after playing bumper cars in the parking lot. He moved away from the damaged vehicles and parked on the other side of the lot. He locked up, swung over the seat, and curled up in the back.

Luke woke at about nine o'clock, the lot near empty. In the distance, he could see a prowl car checking things out. He flung himself behind the wheel. His stomach felt like a bashed head. Wentworth remembered tonight was the poker night at Eagan's. First he had to feed.

He drove to an Indian restaurant on the way to Hans' and tanked up on Tandori Crawfish, Tikka Kebob, Pakora and stuck to drinking beer.

When Eagan saw the stranger at the door, he was not ready to let him in. Wentworth spoke about the last woman he remembered Eagan with.

"What's with the Huron haircut, Luke? Creditors? Your ex-wife?"

No one who knew Wentworth at the game. There were two women playing who looked like sisters, facially. One was obese and the other was ripe. Her armpits?

Luke was seated next to her and he found the smell corroding his less than satisfactory concentration. Several times, it was necessary to remind Wentworth it was his bet. This annoyed everyone, especially the fat-bottomed woman who was losing most of the money.

The two other men were opposites. One was moustached and

a fashion-saloned fop, while the other was in a greasy suit and sweated out small pots. He was out early. No one was willing to take IOUs. The smelly skinny woman became friendlier and friendlier towards Wentworth as the pile before him grew. He was so far from being in control that it seemed he'd be easy to take later.

Luke managed to perceive some of the lady's intentions and changed seats after a new player was introduced. "Here, give you my lucky chair." The new guy stuck his nose up after a few seconds and belligerently demanded that the lady take a shower before the game continued. A trifling argument ensued. The skinny one violently refused to admit she stank. She was voted into the shower by unanimous decision and the game held up for coffee.

Luke had already taken a chunk of everyone's capital and began feeling mild guilt. He decided to violate smart poker practice and began to drink. He'd drop forty or fifty dollars of the two hundred and sixty he was ahead and retire. What actually happened was, instead of dropping, he continued to gain. Luke, sloppier even than before, seriously annoyed the more serious players. His days were so horrible now.

A face-off pot came at three in the morning. The fop raised half a grand. Everyone but Wentworth folded. He matched the pot and raised ten dollars. The moustache was twisted and twirled by nervous fingers and the bet was jumped another grand —more money than Luke had showing on the table. Luke reached in past his gun, put in the cash and called.

When he woke up on Eagan's couch the next morning, he couldn't remember the game. He had been holding four fours to a full house, black aces and red fives.

Hans came over to Wentworth eating an apricot. He had another in hand for the hungry victor.

"Perfect. Try one!" Hans held it under Luke's nose. "Just smell! What a delicious odor!"

"I'm choking!" Wentworth cried springing to his feet. With an effort, he conquered the spasm.

"Nerves?"

"Nerves 2."

Eagan sat down next to the upright friend and went on eating. He spat the apricot stones into his hand, then deposited them on the glass coffee table. Luke sat back down, rubbing a hand over this bald head.

"Quite a show you put on last night," Hans said between mouthfuls.

"Did I lose a lot?"

"Oh, you won quite a lot, but that's not the performance I was referring to," Eagan teased, bit into the fruit.

Luke tried to weather the pause. "OK. What'd I do?"

"Don't you remember? Try and remember."

"All right, Hans. I'm burning. Spill."

"Sure you don't want yours?" Eagan pointed to Luke's apricot.

"No. Help your greedy face to it."

"Never seen you so grumpy, Wentworth. Didn't you sleep well?"

"I dreamt about waking up and immediately cracking open the skull of anyone dumb enough to give me a hard time."

"Oh." Eagan backed away, slumping over the table to count seeds and take occasional nibbles from the soft pale pleasure.

"You coprophilic jack off!" Luke looked closely at the palms of his pained hands. "What is it that I'm supposed to have done?"

"Why, the way you and that gimlet-eyed lady anorexic caroused after the game dissolved."

"We did not!"

"Oh yeah you did—we all saw you."

"Saw me do what?"

"We all took turns at the keyhole. Boy was she greedy and anxious after you'd won that last potful of money."

"It's a lie!"

"Well, yes. How'd you guess? Mean you don't remember slumping over the table reaching for your winnings and just collapsing there? You wouldn't come off the pile until everyone had left and, even then, you took a swing at me when I tried to drag you off it."

"That sounds more like me."

"That is you, Luke. What you want for breakfast?"

"Eggs Benedict?"

"No bacon, no Hollandaise."

"We'll go out. And I'll buy if you drive."

"I've gotta get to work. If you're not ready to move yet, don't forget to lock up on the way out."

"Eagan?"

"Yes, boss?"

"Do you think someone, some group could be plotting to put the present system on its knees?"

"What? Are you kidding? People are plotting to do that day and night."

"Internally, I mean."

"Internally, externally. Everyone wants to divide up the pie a new way. It's never been otherwise."

"How do you figure?"

"My clients demonstrate it to me every day. Television and movies, radio, advertising, publishing and the press—what do you think they really are? Entertainment devices, information distributors? That's secondarily." He took a look at his watch.

"Shit! No more time! See you this afternoon, maybe. Almost through with your case?"

"Almost through."

"Good. We'll go down to Ensenada for a week. You've got some money for a change. Hang onto it."

"Sure."

"Help yourself to anything in the fridge," Eagan chirruped as he left.

Luke felt too exhausted to get up from the table. Losing his nerve again. He was afraid to finish this job. They knew him, he only knew three of them. After sitting a few minutes, Luke decided that it was time for a drink. Only problem, how to get it down. He wandered into the kitchen and threw a few papayas, a grapefruit and some oranges into the blender. Then, vodka. Luke had the concoction to his lips and—his stomach refused it. He heaved it and a load of other glop into the sink and ran the garbage disposal. He put out some vinegar. Coffee, toast, eggs, sausage—the healthy life? Nope. Sex, alcohol, and poker, the track, shooting craps. Luke saw his distorted reflection in the coffee cup and added cream. He was fumbling to try to recognize himself and not be the bald-headed stubby-faced crayfish that seemed to want to grab him. "It's the weather, I suppose." He glanced out of the window and cringed when he got yet another look at himself. "Need some vitamin shots. Have to see the doc soon."

Luke had never questioned what about this line of work still appealed to him. Work must be trotted after without worrying about lightning, hurricane, (San Andreas Fault) fires on the hillsides or nuclear war. Let nothing snatch away your will power or spike your heart to the wall. That was all the philosophy he could use. Luke kept on staring out the kitchen window which, through a cluster of trees, showed you the Hollywood Bowl down below. Luke needed more rest, but feared a sleep in which a jumble of questions, plots, and suspicions would beat him to a pulp. In the bathroom, he found the necessary sedatives to insure a completely blank repose from which he could rise and hurry to finish his task.

XXII. IN WHICH DRANTHUS
TEACHES A LESSON

Dranthus' lecture, given while Luke dozed dreamlessly, was anecdotal that morning. Einstein had refused to accept the theory of the expanding universe, although others had decided that it was so on the basis of Einstein's own equations. Albert had to travel halfway round the world and look through the big California telescope before he was converted. In those days, Albert was still anti-mystical and anti-religious. He didn't want the theologians barging in declaiming their suppositions about creation.

Edgar showed some slides, talked about Billy Blake and ended the screening with photos of the darling "V" shaped sister Hyades, Atlas' daughters, in the Taurus cluster.

The lecture was aimed at intimidating those it would, excite those it should, and to pull in those who thought they could. "Those who can, will. Those who can't, won't." Those who "couldn't" weren't human to him. Beetles who had clever mandibles or falcons who'd pull slower or crippled birds out of the sky. That was all. Not it? Intelligence had, by accident, a human form for now. But that would all soon change.

"One thousand and five hundred years from the fall of Rome to get? People back to mystifying the pettiest trifles and aspects of behavior and personality. Voodoo, yoga, pygmy music, tattoo and pierce my tongue, new-age messiahs. What crap."

Dranthus could rave on to himself for quite a time and at a stunning pace. Most of the problem though was frustration at not being able to satisfy the $nt > 1O14cm-3s$ inequality. That was his real bitch. Physically, this condition is clear enough. The longer the process runs, the less intense the reaction of "burning" may be. Magnetic confinement of plasma might be the simplest feature of a plasma reactor.

Edgar had picked up a splinter while storing the lecture equipment and glided over to student health to have it plucked. Actually, the laser method (as well as electron beam heating) implies ... Dranthus ran the problem over and over again. Tomorrow's lecture was going to be on high-temperature superconductivity. He could already hear himself saying, "the phenomenon of superconductivity was discovered in 1911 and for many years it reamed (no, that's remained, although "reaming" us is what it's still doing) not only inexplicable as the most annoyingly puzzling phenomenon in macrophysics, but pragmatically almost useless." Arghh, arghh, arrghh—"There now," says the doe-faced nurse, "It's out." There seem, in principle, to be no factors hindering the construction of, say, a 300-kOe magnet at helium temperatures. It'll never come out! Where is it! Edgar wants so much to be first in line for a Nobel Prize in 2025.

"Sooner Momma, much sooner," he can remember saying back in, oh, 1986.

Returning from the clinic, Edgar lets the figures of the women in his class drip through his mind. There was a redhead, but she had the cow-eyed look and, although amply uddered, the legs were a bit too fat and, as for the ass—her capillaries were too close to the surface of the skin. What power to captivate she had had better be applied to bringing a medical student or a business boy to heel in a hurry. She probably had pretensions toward the arts. Dranthus could see her cataloging the pretty colors of the dwarf stars he had shown today. The word "dwarf" set off another cycle. He gloated for a moment because his main enemy, the director of research, had just been admitted into the hospital for cancer of the bowel. That magneto- current barrier has been overcome, superconducting materials are available now, but what's the use? Damn it! They can't get enough juice into any of these methods! It must be a long way round or a shortcut through.

Edgar was rounding the corner to his office when, who should be waiting faithfully for him to return so they could "talk" than the red, half-desired one. Dranthus was not above getting them in the office if he needed it. The novelty had not faded. Why, in his teaching assistant days, the closet in his classroom would do.

XXIII. IN WHICH LUKE STILL SEEMS STUCK

L uke could still see at himself reflected in the windowpane, sitting at a table equidistant on the other side of the glass. He tried not to look up from his plate much. Finally, he just changed seats for a view of the kitchen cabinets and stove.

Stuck with him, there's nothing to tell. Memories are floating like dead birds down his river-mind. He's struggled for several minutes for the name of that girl who gave him his first head in high school. Her clit must have been in her tongue, she liked to do it so much. She married the ugliest face in high school, a guy who had an automatic shift in his sports car, but who had horse dick. Luke had gone to the ten year high school reunion. That was when he was still in his white-collar days. Far away, painful as ever to recall. She'd straightened out completely, had seven kids and looked like a kind mother (no alcohol, no pills anymore) from stem to stern. She'd adopted the trim, short-haired completely fulfilled and satisfied small town woman look. Bob was moving up at the bank and the youngest played short-stop on the winning little league team. Bob was not as ugly as Luke remembered. He later found out that a Boston plastic surgeon was responsible for Bob's chin (He never had one before, his face just curving away into his neck). Luke hadn't gone through any of his own transformations yet. He was shown a photograph of the seven children and three of them were decently chinless, defending the trait. (A trust had been set up for all of them so that they could all get chins on their twenty-first birthdays.) Luke wondered if the boys had inherited the other major male characteristic and scrutinized the photo so closely that Arlene asked him what he was looking for.

Gotta get you out of this kitchen, Wentworth. Two pots of coffee and still only dim hope of conscious thought.

He got up to use the can. The coffee flushed him out. He went to find Eagan's phone books to look up Obolus' address.

"Find the girl and end the case," kept on shuttling through the head. A pair of forceps to reach in and pull that phrase out, please! Would finding Alica Poule tidily finish it? Or would Dranthus, Obolus, and Boil have to commit suicide together? Maybe even that wouldn't end Luke's involvement with this union educated lords and snappy killers.

Obolus lived on Apollo Drive, a street surrounded by Olympus, Jupiter, Hermes, Zeus (a coarse repeat that), Achilles, Oceanus, Electra and Venus Drive up Laurel Canyon. Oh, well, that's as good as living in Shangri-La, I suppose.

Wen tried Obolus' number. Not home. He tried the university through the switchboard. There he was. W. pretended a mistaken connection, false voice and hung up. Alone and at home is how Luke was going to serve Oscar up. Drop in after midnight.

Luke was entertaining powerful hopes that Obolus would point like a bloodhound to the location of the missing Poule under brief exposure to the gun.

Went hadn't noticed before. Felt the tinge only. He was shoeless. His left baby toe was a bit mushy in the green and white checker-patterned sport sock. Blood. He'd stepped on a sliver of glass while blindly perambulating around the furniture. He pulled the wet thing off. The stuff was coagulating and turning flaky brown. Luke put an index finger down to edge out the piece of glass. A toast of his bewhiskered lips! *There you go, my heart's abhorrence.* "People actually once thought in Latin just as now they're thinking in German, Greek, Russian and money. Oh, god. Will hell dry me out? Blue-black. Lustrous. Eyes aglow." He dropped the sliver into an imitation jade ashtray.

Eagan actually had a television set discreetly hidden behind a panel in the wall. Luke found out about it one evening when a Ralph Meeker film about detection was on. Eagan couldn't resist making Wentworth watch it. Luke slid opened the panel and exposed the nineteen color inches. No schedule or newspaper, so Luke diced with the channels. Listening to the pitches, Wentworth was sourly reminded of the feeling he had on that carnival ride named "The Zipper" that Jenny had lured him onto. Around and around, centrifugal force, like a gerbil on a treadmill. Well, when was it? Only four years ago. He snapped the conspiracy off, closed shop, and began hunting for either a sedative or a drink.

L.W. found both, but opted to rejoin the lotus eaters. Ashe was passing out, he fused his two best friends together. Tad, who ended up in the hospital after passing out at a bus depot—didn't want to go home to the wife and family. Declared a victim of personality disintegration by the docs. And Willy, who revolved in and out of detox centers unable to stomach his payable bills. One torso, two heads, and three legs. Huh. Luke had set the alarm for eleven o'clock and wrote a note for Hans not to wake him. He was safe on second. All he had to do, since there were still no outs, was to wait for a well hit single to send him home.

XXIV. MEANWHILE

Boil's mitochondrion were misbehaving. Alica had bitten the poor boy in dismal half with the Janus-faced manner she had mastered. Lucky for Boil he hadn't ever encountered the maturer version. J.P. was a magnification 20 compared to A.P's piddling 10 +3-00.07. Each of us has some courage but, zap, smash, a bad night in a shooter's motel, and what then? The normally docile and catalytic enzymes in uncentralized revolution. Boil's hands were shaking. The graduate students were greedy to notice it.

Boil had never been "slow." He should have dismissed the class. Instead, he tried to conjure some of the old professional magic. In other words, he told one of the students to try the experiment to see if he could make it a success. The choice was Boil's usual astute one. The obviously bright, but clumsy on stage, student blundered things much worse than Boil. The recombinant DNA demonstration was over. Boil dryly mocked the "human factor" that had botched many a potential day of progress in the history of science. The fox had again eluded the barking hounds by ducking into a network of slyly dug holes.

The overwhelmingly impressive feature of Aloysius'

personality was that he didn't let momentary triumphs erase the army of more important problems trying to oppress him. Boil is too bright for me. When you start to bring in electron microscopes and digitizers that measure and map DNA fragments projected in a darkroom from a photograph and it all has to do with tracing the dispersion and paths of human sperm, you've left me behind. Let me wake up Luke. He's flying over the Aswam Dam looking for Pharonic statues. He's easy to absorb and comprehend. Let's put away our laser scalpels.

XXV. IN WHICH
WENTWORTH'S SLEEP IS
INTERRUPTED

L uke was awoken by an agitated mumbling coming from out of the wall. Eagan's television set had a timer and Luke turned it off right. Walter Brennan was telling his nephew that he wasn't going to let the tenant use the unplanted acres for peanut production. Peanuts weren't ever going to get anybody anywhere.

It was five-fifteen. Wentworth gave Obolus another ring. Not there. Luke was still for surprising Oscar at home. He smelled something funny. What was it? He held a hand in front of his mouth. Awful breath. What was that from? His foot was infected too. Luke decided to clean up. Although, while ransacking the medicine cabinet, Luke found some mouthwash, he decided to leave his breath alone and share it with Oscar. A key was being turned in the lock. Luke had left the gun tucked under his coat on the couch. Uncomfortable.

It was jolly Hans Eagan returned with grocery sacks. Hans asked Luke to go out and bring in the bottle of wine left on the front seat. Wine? Good wine? Sure. Hans had garnished fifty dollars from Luke's winnings and had gone out and stocked up. An aspiring actress, partially promoted by his agency, was coming over to be served a king-crab and fixings for supper. It was rumored, extensively rumored, that she wouldn't go less than three ways. Eagan had smoked her out about the meal that afternoon (he was quite the cook), knowing that loopy Luke would still be available to help execute the plan.

"Luke, you can't miss out on this. No, goddamnit. You're staying. I even bought your favorite wine."

"But I've got to get over to—"

"It can wait. Have a drink and limber up. She'll be here in an hour. If you leave now, I'll never let you back at my table again."

"Your dinner table?"

"No, dolt! My poker table. Argh! What's that smell?"

"Me."

"Get rid of it. Now!"

What could Luke do? He resigned himself to Eagan's monomania. He hoped that next time things would work out so that he couldn't feel pressured, tempted.

The fun started. Eagan anxiously commanded Luke to answer the door. He, Hans, was up to his armpits in Salad Nicoise. There was the woman all right, but with her aged agent. Eagan must have either given the wrong signals or been so obnoxious that she judged fatherly protection necessary.

The agent was a messy affair. Suit out of mode and unshined shoes. Luke offered to escort the radiance and her curious escort to the kitchen to meet the salad monster. Harry, the agent became sullen. It was a matter of whether or not the chef was using a microwave in there. The agent had a steel plate in his head. An aging starlet had thrown and dented his head with the fake Oscar he was trying to impress her with. Plus, he had a pacemaker. The overwork involved in peddling medium to no-talent had caused heart attacks.

Eagan was distinctly unhappy to see Harry. Hans had planned dinner for three, and three afterwards. Crab-meat and rich wine were out for Hare. His triglycerides would shoot out of orbit and he'd crash down dead. Harry would stick to tomatoes and salad, a piece of dry bread and conversation about Glenda's chances for getting the lead in the sequel being planned for the multi-billion dollar science fiction bug-hunt slime-fest. Eagan was crude about her chances. He could only see her on the small screen. Harry wanted to know about Luke. Strangers made him sanction his doubts and validate his anxieties.

Although he didn't look the part, Luke presented himself as son of a Dallas box manufacturer in L.A. to scout new territory. "Boxes? Was that all the company made?" A subsidiary made the staples that held the boxes together. An offshoot was raising catfish in Brazil and buffalo in the Argentine. "Buffalo?" Good meat. Cheap and easy to raise. With meat prices sure to go up as more people on the planet demanded their share of protein, buffalo were a sound investment. Three ranches, 30,000 head already started. Be on the market in four months. The hoofs made better gelatin than horse or cow. Herds swarming over the Pampas. His company very popular with the gauchos.

Harry and Glenda were, like, glum and glummer. It was not movie-talk. Luke drank three shares of wine. Eagan's hadn't given up. He concentrated on making the phone ring, call the agent away, and make the small star shine between the two of them.

The phone "*baaaarrringggg*" rang. Harry said he always left word where he would be. Dr. Hunch, they tried to call him, but only "Hare" (as in hare-brained) stuck. "Sorry, Glenda, but my special effects wizard's been electrocuted. Gotta replace him tonight. Enjoy the meal."

"Can't they resurrect?" asked the sloshed box man.

"Resuscitate, you mean?"

"Don't worry about us. Do you remember how to get to the highway from here?"

"Two lefts and a right? Bye, Glenda. My wife is there and she's not strong about these kinds of things. Be good," Hare said to the boys.

Eagan wondered how he conjured these miracles and poured wine before showing Hunchy remorse, regret, and the door.

Glenda was soused. Luke decided she'd be no joy and decided to give Obolus another try. Oscar was home. Luke apologized. Wrong number in a dopey Dallas accent. He returned to the table. Hans was pouring coffee and praising his hand at desserts. Glenda was trying to beg off. Her diet. And she wised. A widespread "appetite," she was. She acted morose.

Hans pretended not to have intuited her feelings. It was sadly hopeless and after the strawberry roll was served (Glenda devoured hers while Eagan only listlessly poked at his), he offered to drive her home. She wanted to see a movie on T.V. Starting soon. Could she watch it there and be driven home later? Groan. Eagan resigned himself to a cheerless night. His agony intensified when he witnessed Wentworth arming himself. Wen already had both shoes on after the barefoot meal.

XXVI. PAGES OF VIOLENT DEATH AND CYNICAL MURDER

Luke wondered about the dents in the car. After awhile, he remembered. But, stumbling around for the information, he came across a dream he'd had in college. Studying till five in the morning for a chemistry exam. He'd been searching for a formula in the textbook concerning bonding molecular orbitals, except it wasn't his familiar textbook. The books he had to search through contained all kinds of information, from dinner menus to Jacobite drawings in garish colors of the execution of the king. Things were mixed up in other words. Neptunes with sherbet spoons in their hands instead of tritons and riding in open carriages down the bois. Pulled by oxen instead of seahorses, that kind of twisted around. Looking for what seemed hours, Luke found the recipe tucked between opposing ads for a pornographic novel and bee-keeping equipment. Luke wrote the steps on a slip of paper while keeping the index finger of his left hand planted solidly on the signs—gloriously happy that his labor had ended now he could sleep.

Luke slipped the piece of paper in his shirt pocket for safekeeping. He was sleeping in his clothes that night to get an early start on coffee in the morning. But when he woke up in the morning, the paper was gone. He got a "C" on the test and transferred shortly thereafter into management.

Here we are at Obolus' house. Apollo Drive number 1848. Luke drives past, parks three blocks away and stalks back.

Wentworth sneaks around the side, to sliding doors that are/are-not locked? Not locked and with the curtains drawn across them except for a quarter-inch slit Luke can peer through. He gets belly down on the brick patio and cases what's going on in the living room.

Obolus is in an easy chair surrounded by nearly a dozen cats all rolled over on their backs in a fit of drippy ecstasy.

Oscar is reading a *Cat in the Hat* story to them. Luke snickers at the sentiment, but remains bewildered by the overturned cats. Obolus hears something.

"Who's there?"

Luke pushes himself up. He parts the tinted glass and steps through the doors with the most sardonic grin he can muster.

"Who are you?"

"Where's Alica Poule?"

Oscar chuckles a smidgen upon recognizing this bizarre version of the sloppy (to his mind), dog-bright detective. Oscar hasn't been clued about Luke's dispatching of the black carred, now charred, triad. He's about to find out Luke's not the lovable pet of former meeting. The gun is produced accompanied by the repetition of the Wentworth question. Oscar protests ignorance. *FFttt.* The statue of a plaster cat on Oscar's writing desk fragments. Oscar doesn't think too much of the demonstration. Luke's a fine marksman though, don't you think? The cats seem to be purring their agreement and are not bothered by the loss of their painted Egyptian brother.

Now cats are supposed to love the smell of petrol and oil, opium smoke, (which these cats seemed familiar with and Obolus had tried once, he being a fashionable professor—but it gave him a vision of himself revolving endlessly through deep space, a skeleton in an electric chair with a madman's grimace still recognizable on the fleshless jaw. No more of that), yeast (bread baking was more in Oscar's line), freshly slaughtered meat (but more of that later), the chlorinated smell of household washing, plaster (fresh, wet stuff not the splintered kind), fennel, ammonia, very Frenchly the smell of stagnant water in vases, perfumes, the draw of sexual odors and food.

Obolus had some interesting species of cats. Two caught Luke's eye, a red Abyssian male named Rum and a black rumpie female minx named Agrippina. There was Tom Quartz—named after Teddy Roosevelt's cat who had himself been named after a Mark Twain character. (I've always thought that intelligent folk devote too much time to this kind of sentimental naming, but they do, and so here's Oscar's group of cats) An amicable Persian; Dusty, a British Blue (Not Duster Bennet); Peta, a sulking (normally) Siamese; Zoroaster, an Angora; Tibs, an alleycat found wandering the campus; and Cognac, who we first met in Oscar's office.

Luke shot Zoroaster first. Oscar screamed and screamed. Luke backed up and closed the sliding doors. He went over and turned up the stereo to out-do Obolus. Oscar calmed and wanted to talk. Talk was what Luke wanted to hear. Zoroaster had gotten it in the neck. The body flung itself through the air against the wall where the pumping heart was gushing blood in shorter and shorter, quieter and quieter spurts, onto a polar bear rug.

Luke only wanted one thing, "I want to hear Alica Poule's

name her current location and that's it."

Obolus started raving economics to Wenty—market verses product orientation, trusts, the destructive synergistic effect of conglomerate fusion of vitally distinct resources and a stream of unconvertible mish-mosh. Tom Quartz was hit *fffft*. A little too high in the head. The cat's dazed look resolved. Tom wobbled to his feet, began to chase himself in tight circles, then slumped down in a corner, heaving up mucous, vitals, and blood.

Imagine Oscar shrieking. Up went the stereo. For mercy's effect Luke put another shot into the slowly dying Quartz. Oscar wanted to talk again. Down went the decibel level of the popular music.

It was again all about economics—the inflation, `71 gold scandal debacle, selling out of the country to foreign money. Cognac never moved. Luke hit him in the heart then splattered Agrippina with two or three shots across much of the nearest wall. The remaining cats were trying to struggle to alertness. Up went the stereo. Oscar was slumped in a chair tearing his hair out and biting his knuckles, muttering over and over again in a dim voice, "Why doesn't he understand? Why doesn't he want to understand?"

Luke was definitely peeved. Obolus seemed beyond range. What was Luke going to do now? No time to think! Obolus had gotten up from the easy chair, grabbed a paperweight from the writing desk and was running at Luke to crush his skull. Luke put a shot into Obolus' knee and the professor slammed down on Peta (his least favorite, anyway). Bleeding, hysterical and unable to revenge himself on Luke who had already slid out of the door, Obolus crashed the marble egg (repeatedly) on Peta's skull. Now he was a murderer too.

After a half hour of sobbing and trying to stop the bleeding, Obolus called Boil to tell him about Luke's destruction and about the detective's new guise. Boil knew a doctor who could be trusted and Obolus was not to do anything by himself.

This last order powdered Oscar's remaining ego completely. When Boil and Dr. Tropp arrived, they found (after an annoying search and much cursing), Oscar hanging from an overhanging pipe in the basement. He'd used thin wire and by now it had cut to the bone so that the head was dangling from a few strands of muscle over the back of the body. The corpse was almost empty of blood and in this condition there was too much mess, so Boil and Tropp left everything as it was, concocting alibis as they scurried to the doctor's Mercedes.

Luke hadn't driven off after leaving Oscar. He wanted to make sure the oaf didn't die on him. When he saw Boil and the doctor arrive (he could tell it was a doctor by the caduceus on the license plate and the black bag) from across the street in the oak tree he had climbed, he thought that everything was going to be all right. They weren't even calling in any law. But why were they so highly agitated leaving Obolus' house?

Luke descended the tree to go back in and resume his visit with Oscar. He presumed to find him wrapped up in bed. Wentworth hated the smell of drying blood. It was so strong it had a flavor to it. You could taste it in the air. It took Luke less than half the time it had taken Boil and the Doc to discover Obolus' whereabouts. Uh-oh. Let's try and figure out where we stand here. Let's get out of the house, wiping fingerprints off the sliding door (can't remember what else was touched), anyway. Wentworth had never had control slip so far away before. Unexplored territory. Terrible incognita. Frightened by what might grow in the climate. Spacing.

XXVII. IN WHICH THERE ARE DISCUSSIONS AND DECISIONS MADE

B oil was shaken up and furious. The description Obolus had given of Luke didn't help much. The obvious thing was that Luke had only two other places to go to get the information he wanted. What could be done? Tropp tried to answer Boil that the police would be able to handle Wentworth. "Well, that would be like telling the families of prospective patients that you frequently botched operations high on drugs." Tropp understood immediately. What could they do? The head of their terrorist arm was called, Wentworth described. Naturally, the description was flimsy, probably inaccurate, and gave the false impression Luke was smarter than he was. Three good men already sacrificed over some babe Boil had emptied himself into.

Boil worried over having to report these facts. It occurred to him that the terrorist arm, which was by no means under his power or jurisdiction, would come across with another solution to the Wentworth problem.

Luke himself was not for having himself made into target

practice for a fledgling outfit. He drove over to the medical technologist's. She was just back from a luau and sleepy. She had difficulty in believing that this was her former night's Romeo. Luke looked like warmed up pasta, pasty-faced and haggard. How did he lose all his hair in just a few days? Lawn mower ran over him while he was snoozing on the grass in a public park.

Even his wit was had it.

Luke asked for a razor. She actually had some around for boys who stayed the night, liked it in the morning, and had to rush right to the office.

Wentworth got rid of the beard and trimmed it down to a moustache. He again became someone else. Barb came up behind him and rubbed his newly shaven head. "It'll grow back won't it?" she purred. Purring made Luke nervous. To calm his nerves he took a bath and invited Barb in. After a few minutes, Luke's fingers went exploring. Giggles. There were protestations that the water made it dry and that the glands secrete lubricant in the bath. Barb wanted to roll out of the tub and onto the floor. Luke suggested Vaseline in place of that. No, she wanted to do it naturally. Luke found himself mostly stimulated by the temperature of the tub.

They reached a compromise. Onto the floor for awhile with delicate foreplay to be administered by a gymnastically precise tongue and then back to the water. Luke's moustache tickled and Barb squirmed and moved and finally moaned. She almost hit her head on the sink pipes but Luke pulled her back. Made aware of the great hurt that had been spared her, she consented to return tubwards earlier than agreed.

Barb grabbed onto the faucet handles with her hands (she knew this fantasy was going to wear down her knees) and Luke licked and rogered her for a pleasant long while before collapsing.

They showered together, continuing to exchange gifts of attention and affection for another half an hour. Barb began to ask Luke questions about the case he was on, but Luke refused comment until offered food. French toast and sausages?

Barb prepared the guslar's banquet while the deceiver investigated even stranger territory of his new face. Still looking tired and crummy.

Barb was in a shortie, see-through nightie. Luke remained bare: ate, drank a pot of coffee, asked for a cigarette and, with his engine tuned, proceeded to tell the following tale.

About a week and a half ago, a millionaire in his sixties enlisted Wentworth to find his missing Philipino amanuensis for him. The missing woman was in her early twenties and had a partial daddy complex. That's why they were together. He was putting his money into kelp farming. This guy figures she's off screwing someone else and wants to know who, where and the likes, doesn't much care if she comes back.

"Jealous, isn't he?"

"Very."

Anyway, it's a chase around Los Angeles. This four-foot eleven sugar puss with naturally nice melons isn't going with any one guy. She's got about seven or eight that she visits all the time. The woman's into having an orgasm at least every three hours.

"Well, why all the fuss, why all the disguises, Luke?"

Most of the guys she's screwing know about her affair with the millionaire but don't know about one another. She's been promising them all the moon.

"But they've been getting her moon," Barb laughs.

"Not enough, not enough. These guys are all losers of one sort or another. Youngsters with solid traps of their own to set, they're out for an easy killing." She's been promising them all things that she can't deliver: trips, cars, fulfillment of their every dream and ambition.

"But why the…?"

She found out that I had everything she's doing mapped out. She's got two or three of these guys convinced that I have to be killed or what she's telling them can't come true.

"But won't a phone call to the old man just blow all her cover?"

He's in Hong Kong investigating artificial shrimp, oyster, and more kelp beds. Won't be back for another week. She's the only other office staff. Lives in his house. There's no way to get him a message without going through her. "Couldn't you just call Hong Kong?" Can't do that either. He's travelling under a forged passport and an alias to convince these Hong Kong businessmen that he's an investor. If he told them who he really was, they'd know he was only there to steal and spy.

"Boy, Luke, what a pickle!"

Luke looked deeply into Barb's eyes and suggested bed. Her eyes brightened but a quarter hour later Luke was sawing logs. Barb got dressed to go out and not waste the time. After all, what would her life be if she only spent her life in the lab preparing slides? Barb was thinking, as she motored to a favorite hangout, that love was a dangerous flower. One must go up to the edge of the precipice, tie off, and jump! (and she had acrophobia). Apart from ridicule, love is always shadowed by the fear of being betrayed and permanently scarred. No. Love was not for her. Pleasure was a more relaxed, satisfactory avenue of affairs. What did love ever have on pleasure? The corpses at the office never knew. Danger cultured the only interesting beings.

Luke, a real man of danger and violence, was home in her bed. More exciting than the rest, but still not enough. From what she'd seen, hard companies birth soft men. Experience.

It took her less than twenty minutes to choose someone in the bar. Only a few more decades before humans became absolutely useless. Less than commodities to be bought, traded, and sold. Working with the scientists, Barb hurried. She knew.

A volunteer, just done with a toughening up program in the Foreign Legion (Incidentally, they still have their unofficial harem of whores who travel with them wherever they fight. Not in many places now. They've been turned into paratrooping commandos) was assigned to kill Wentworth. Maybe you've found yourself a worthy adversary, Luke.

What's the youngster been doing? As soon as he was assigned the case, Nathan (one of numerous aliases) got over to Luke's place and rigged a bomb in the oven. Turn on the stove, and you've made "Avec Morte Luke Ala Gelignite."

Next, Nate drove to Petite Center to see the little ex-missus. Ingrid came to the door drunk and in a half-open terry cloth robe. Upon regarding the friendly caller, she perked up a bit. Nate showed her identification that made him "FBI". Nate looked right. A clean-cut looking dude always seems safe, authorial, unapproachable. If Ingrid had watched more television, maybe she would have known that FBI agents work in pairs.

Nate found out in a fairly civil manner that Ingrid didn't know where her sonofabitch ex-husband ("oh, excuse me,") was. He was close to being behind on an alimony payment. She hadn't been able to get hold of him for days, not since he'd taken the kid.

Across town, Edward, back from his aborted sail to Hawaii, wanted to do right by Luke (He'd seen salvation falling drunkenly overboard, nearly eaten, and almost drowned). But Luke wasn't in. Waiting, Ed began to desire a cup of mint tea.

Nate worked quickly, so his next destination was the Poule

property. He got to the locked gate and opened it with a really neat electronic scrambler. Nate wanted to clock how long it would take him from assignation of assignment to completion. He wore a gadget Japanese watch that buzzed on the hour, pressuring him to remember that the hands of time were his immortal enemies. He drove up to the front of the house without forewarning, surveyed the place, and walked around the corner of the house. There he met a group of lazing guard dogs who tried to do their duty. Nate mace 'em. Since that made them howl in pain, Nate slit all their throats with a razor knife.

Poule was conducting his usual gathering when Nate walked in. He went up to the nearest lady, the wistful-eyed, round and firm Latino. He put an arm around her, stood her up and put his knife to her throat.

"Anyone here know where Luke Wentworth is? Quick, I'm psychotic and I'll need to slit this woman's throat if I don't get an answer in five seconds," he charmingly grinned.

"How did you get in here?" Jack shouted.

Nate drew blood.

"He's out looking for my daughter, Alica."

"Where?"

"Don't know."

"Does he call in regularly?"

"Not anymore. He's gone a bit crazy the last few days. Says people have been trying to kill him. His daughter's here. Do you want her?"

Nate let the unsteady woman collapse to the floor and reached for a glass of wine, carefully tasting it. From the far door of the room, the new security guard (grandly athirst to prove himself) ran in, gun searching a target. Nate ducked under the table. The guard's first shot slammed into a Dali lithograph, one of the ones from the musical flower series. The guard tried a second shot. Through the roast beef sitting at center. But that didn't do any damage until someone (I think the new girl) bit into it later and broke a tooth. Nate popped up like a weasel from his burrow and put a tranquilizer dart from a CO_2 gun into the guard's arm. Nate had a more powerful tool available and, obviously, he was not adverse to murder. Don't leave a trail? The room had emptied and Nate had to go searching around for the treacherous Poule.

Jack he found in the study on the phone about to report the vital statistics. He was asked to hang up. Nate went to Poule, grabbed him by the collar and dragged him out to the fishpond where Nate quietly, and without an angry word, held Jack's head under water for a time. The carp looked quizzically at their master's face. It was the first time he'd ever visited.

Nate, after tolerating Poule's squawks and begging, left Jack beside the pond and returned to the study. Nate noticed Poule's collection of toys and scooped them off the desk into his pockets. Nate left a trail of them out of the house and down the drive. He saved a few and shoved them into the glove compartment.

Well, this is who Luke must deal with. What do you think?

Earlier this day, drove to Vegas. Nate read about the explosion at Wentworth's former home. The body, the newspaper reported, wasn't immediately identifiable. There'd be a few days before identification based on dental plates could confirm who the blast victim was.

Nate phoned the story in to his chief. They'd call if needed. "Why don't you go down to the gulf and go fishing for a few days? We have a boat you can use."

"I'm going camping and fishing in the North woods. I'll call when I get back. Is there any spectacular hurry?"

"Not anymore."

XXVIII. WENTWORTH'S ACTIVITIES ON THE DAY JUST DESCRIBED

Ingrid woke Wentworth on her way out to work. She looked tired and Luke wondered why. He'd had a fine night's sleep. He felt rested, his mind clear. Because of what had happened with Obolus, a few days out of town wouldn't hurt.

Driving to the nearest discount store, Luke outfitted himself with some grisly looking polyester print shirts, slacks, a white belt with matching shoes, sunglasses and a felt hat. He thought it time to expose himself to a new set of assumptions. As Luke started across the desert, the hip manifesto about existence and time passed through his head. It excused many things (he was drinking vodka and chewed a Quaalude). "In some remote corner of a universe, glimmering among other innumerable solar systems, there once was a star on which some highly clever organisms (we must go beyond animals to characterize the full measure of the H4He effect) invented truly complex and ingenious survival mechanisms. There was a moment called "world history." Many voices babbled about it. After a few breaths, the star expired and the clever things disappeared. Fortunately, men and women do not balk at being deceived or damaged by this deception. A nerve stimulus gets turned into an image, an image imitated, etc. Every con originates through our equating unequals.

Luke puffs cigarettes, unbuttons shirt buttons, swigs on alcohol, hopes the car can take this steady 100 mph across the desert. What then is "tooth" but a molar army of metonyms and anthropomorphisms? Oh Luke, you're drunk. To be a toothful means using the cut a merry metafarts to Ed Lear. In Nature, the sensory stimuli usually come in over a large number of adjacent neuronal fibers. When interneurons are required (there are lots of them), and each has input connections with axons clutching sensory neurons … But here is Luke driving along, moving his leaden mouth behind the wheel, trying to inhibit them all. It isn't hard to stop people from thinking, but try to stop worrying. Luke was afraid of a return to L.A. and he wasn't in Vegas yet. The gun was in the glove compartment because he'd become shy of it. He was paying cash for all his expenses. In fact, he'd tortured his credit cards in the restroom gas station beyond recognition. What if he lost all his money at the tables?

Wentworth was luckier than he knew. The police were having to assume it was the dick that had been charcoaled. The dental records, which should have been able to identify him, had lately been burned in a fire. This was no accidental fire. No fire of coincidence. L.W.'s dentist, Dr. Zhan, was a sporty, active man in his late sixties who had died whilst playing polo. A horse's hoof clipped his skull after he'd taken a spill. Dr. Zhan's secretary was bribed. Half the owed total bill of an unidentified junior executive with already Alpine debts, to scorch the patient records. From a mouth of crumbling crowns Dr. Zhan had performed miracles (but at quite a cost) in the service of his art.

The doctor's demise was quite a break for the climber and fortunately, the aging secretary needed a quick fix, too.

Luke, look at the stars in the clear desert sky. That red one glimmering over there. Never mind. That's a Cessna landing at the Vegas municipal airport. You're close to the green now. Slow down before you're stopped. How would that look on the front page of the *Times* or the hick *Herald*? So, what makes you think— Hey! Watch out for the pothole!

Wentworth parked and found a coffee shop. He pumped down two club sandwiches and six cups of java to get himself ready for play. The strip reminded him of one of his less oppressive nightmares. He kept on forgetting how he looked. And, really, he looked perfect.

At a black-jack table, Luke found himself a hundred and fifty dollars down after holding his own for awhile. Up carouse two mid-western boys. The taller one, with pimples and greasy hair, beats the dealer three times in a row, so Luke decides he'll go with him. The shorter blond companion loses anyway and drops out. Luke and the gilded one each start to climb several hundred, then one thousand five hundred. A crowd gathers to gawk. The one really dorky looking player (Luke) and the average small-town kid (Tom Hubbel, Clinton, Iowa) take the house down a millionth of an inch. Up two thousand one hundred. The house calls in a new dealer. Changing shifts. Yeah, sure. The new dealer reads "Charlie" on the name tag. Luke scents a monster. It has a crew cut and short, stubby fingers. He picks up the deck. Quicker than the fox can grab a hen. They don't see it. The two kids, the gawkers. Luke sees. Wonders, "How does he get so good?"

Charlie's dad, Morgan, the depression. Skill poor on top of being land dispossessed. Dad had taken to eating insects for a time to stay alive. He wanted to impress upon his son the importance of learning a trade so that if things went sour again, he would not have to eat bugs. To ingrain this possible circuit around the potentially shrinking waist of life, Morgan locked little Charlie in the root cellar for a week and fed him spiders and cockroaches. He let the lad out only when he promised to learn how to cheat at cards.

Cards came naturally to the kid. He practiced two hours a day in the hayloft until he was old enough to deal in Vegas. (You could never get him to open the door of the root cellar again.)

After losing, along with Tom, five hands in a row (and Luke kept his bets small, already fearing that he was facing a doomsday machine), Luke dropped out completely and remained two grand to the good. The crowd was surprised. Luke definitely looked the easier mark of the pair. In fact, Luke could have passed for the dumbest mark in town.

Tom hung on until he'd dropped it all back into the well he had drawn it from, plus a grand and a half more. He wanted to beat this particular dealer, Charlie. Beat Charlie. Wentworth admired Tom's mulishness and conferred with buddy, Aaron, about the how and wherefore of Tom's, uh, stubbornness. After the forty five minutes it took to make Tom stop trying, Luke and Aaron knew all about one another.

Aaron (Himmel) was a surrealist painter of mid-western life. Harware store owners wore pig necklaces and smoked reefer. Women played bridge with satanic Tarot decks while drinking blood from their teacups. Luke was a game salesman for a small software company. Aaron saw the stranger in one of his future compositions. A friendship was struck up. The two Midwesterners from a cement mill town, being near-alcoholics and both chain smokers, accepted Luke's offer to stand drinks.

The ludes were wearing off. Luke and Aaron listened while Tom obsessively relived his time at Charlie's table. They kept ordering Tom doubles in hopes that he would soon be too screwed up to talk.

Luke drew his finger across the gaudy casino floor and spoke. "The Abortion gone mad. The hatred of knowledge, spirit and sensuality." Dressed and looking as he did, Aaron was in awe. How could such a grotesque could be capable of making such an acute observation? Such is reserved for the artistic elite, isn't it? If Luke was saying this about the casino, Aaron wanted to get Luke going about his job. What did the game salesman think about his work?

But Luke had snuck another pill, finished half his vodka on the rocks, and held forth, instead, on the topic of numbers.

"What do you guys think about numbers? Does man invent or merely discover?

They didn't respond. Wentworth hadn't expected more. He called over the bartendress (dressed in a blue and black cowboy) to pour more drinks. Maybe they needed another round or two before he punched on. The boys clutched the drinks tightly, listened intermittently. Luke interrupted himself several times, trying to catch their minds when their egos weren't smothering them. I don't remember how many times he caught them—only that he was buying the drinks.

"Every number has a persona. An individual nemesis it strives against. Opposites or just other numbers with bad characters. Ones that don't fit in. Seven is an oily slick number. Either of you like to shoot dice? Well, seven is oily, rich, and slick. Three is lumpy. An old couch with worn springs. An aunt you don't like or a carnival ride operator who's just smart enough to give young kids the evil eye. Five. Pale. Round as a beach ball. With a handle that invites you to lift it. Disappears when you reach for it. Four's bread. Soft, doughy, yeasty and white. Six's a fat cake with heavy white frosting, layered with spiced jellies. Say, I'm getting hungry again. Seems like I just ate a little while ago. Two's, of course, a swan with its neck folded in that curve of a squat church bell. Twelve must be more delicate, a piece of blown glass. Nine. Nein. No, nine. Like the tilted note of a kettle drum. Seventy-two seems like a piece of heavy rock. Granite for a building. Thirty-three's dirty. Sixty-six is like a woman's make-up kit. Say, I've run out of gas."

"That's forty-four," Tom wisecracked.

"What are these games you sell?" Aaron asked.

Wentworth stared as if Aaron had asked a state secret. A buzzing blankness started to hammer nails into Luke's brain. Later, it would suck the contents out.

The proud representative declared that his company's product, "Masturbates the dreams of those from eight to eighty-seven."

Tom spluttered into his drink.

"Weren't working backwards. Now at age two. In another year, we'll own you before you can get out of the womb. Hey, fellows, do you really still think I'm a hick?"

The two put on embarrassed expressions.

"I'm duded up like this because of a bet I made with our stallion over-salesman in Detroit. You boys only get into town today?"

"Yes."

"Well, our convention was here for a week, left yesterday, and Lester and I made the bet on Thursday. He'd better pay up. If he welches…!" He raised his arm along with his voice and it summoned the bartendress. As long as she was here, one more time all `round.

"Is your name really Arnold?" asked Aaron getting comfortable.

"No, it's Alice. Actually it's Richard, Richard Parrott." Bird jokes flew around for a tedious long while, the two stopping to invite Luke to their hotel room for further refreshment and to make up for their "Pretty Polly" leg pulling.

Tom was tense from losing most of his money, except for $543.27, or so. Tom still continued to turn inwards. Aaron and Luke began scheming a way to pull Tom away from his masochistic meatheadness. Replay. Replay. Replay. We should have a mediation in here about the nature and/or essence of time ala Proust, Joyce, or Nabokov, but this is just a piddly genre novel so, no use trying any of that. Two days ago, my friend's kid's girlfriend got killed by a junkie out on parole who nodded off behind the wheel. "What day was that?" Is there much hope of ever being able to keep track of any of it? And if we don't try to? Stuck, aren't we.

While thumbing through the yellow pages in the motel room (you could hear Tom talking to himself in the toilet and punching himself after back talking a strong self-rebuke) for a pizza, Aaron came upon "female escorts." He summoned Luke over to judge the quarter, half, and full-page spreads.

They commiserated for a while. After agreeing to stake Tom to his shot, they phoned the folks with the largest ad.

The voice on the phone promised speedy delivery. Tom came out of the john asking if they'd found a pizza place yet. Himmel and Parrott squawked that something better was on its way, but would not tell poor Tom what.

"Can't be better than food in your gut," Tom protested. Insisting that it was "far better" than food, Tom guessed quickly as to what kind of call they'd made. "I still want a pizza!" He told Aaron to throw him the phone book. Tom made a choice of his own. Large with sausage, pineapple, and green peppers.

"Blech!" Peptic ulcer, anyone?

The five-foot-six man arrived with a portfolio of Polaroid

dates. Everyone is encouraged to indulge his personal appetite. Aaron wanted the exceptional face, Tom the one with good love handles. Luke knew the vendor wouldn't deliver the requested goods, so he chose an older and almost tired looking angel. It was eighty dollars a throw, one hundred and twenty each for Aaron and Parrott. The man in the lacquer suit and polished alligator shoes, expressed pleasantness upon being shown the inspiring fields of green. With the cumbersome album folded under his arm, he exited.

Tom and Aaron began debating who would entertain his date where. Luke approached the bathroom mirror to see if he could plead a case for his former looks. No dice. He wondered if borrowing a shirt would soften his appearance much. Then he remembered that Aaron was short and Tom was thin and shoulderless.

The pizza arrived first. It was hot because of the truck's portable oven. Tom had forgotten to order cold drinks. The tap water tasted like birdlime and straight alcohol was poor companion to hot sausage. The green peppers had been forgotten and Tom haggled for a reduction. He didn't get it.

The ladies arrived. What Luke had anticipated, cold and without allure. Tom and Aaron were amazed that they could have been so venally deceived. One was young and tight, Angela. She walked through the door flicking snot off the end of her finger back into the parking lot. The other two were _____. The more experienced one, Lola, thought she recognized a kindred spirit in Wentworth. The other, Nora, immediately sat on the couch and awaited the questions.

The eighty dollar fee was "an introduction." For anything else … Hubbel and Himmel were daemonically displeased. Wentworth controlled his bemusement. The plumply bunned and expanding Nora pulled a nail file from her purse and began sawing her way through this prisoner's dilemma.

The boys felt (gulping and gnawing pizza carnivorously) cheated. They wouldn't pay another F'ing dime for the goods. What were they going to do? What were they going to do? Himmel made a rudely truthful comment about Lola's nose. The ladies exchanged a cue, and got up to leave.

"We have friends in this town," said Nora examining her nails. "You can't push around who's behind us."

The Hubbel-Himmel protested against this arrangement. Luke relaxed in a recliner and played spectator. *Whoosh!* There went a grim threat. A vindictive epithet whizzed by. It was agreed the sleazy old stars would have to be thrown out. "But they're leaving anyway." Post-war days. The johns in uniform come back to find out they've been betrayed. They'll always be betrayed. "No they're not! Lock 'em in the bathroom!" The trio bolted for the door, but Aaron waved them back with a serrated plastic knife.

Tom called the manager of the service. Bitter bickering. Who had violated what claims? "You violated a verbal contract," came shooting out from between Tom's gapped teeth.

"And we've got the girls locked in the bathroom. You won't be able to make any more money with them until we let them out." The alligator promised to come right over.

Tom and Aaron began to chatter about how they, in fact, may be dealing with syndicated goods. Their concern infected Wentworth. His gun was miles away. The mace. Gone! No. There. Safe. Ready.

Tom and Aaron Chipped and Daled around the room cursing their cupidity. Tom was especially angry because he hadn't even paid for this trouble. "This is worse than the missing peppers!"

Possible weapons were sought. Tennis rackets. Tom and Aaron positioned themselves, poised like butterfly hunters on either side of the door. A spray of machine gun bullets was feared. Would they buzz through the wood and leave their bodies disgustingly maimed and bloodied?

Luke remained where he was and monopolized the gin. (The couch was not in the line of fire.)

Twenty minutes of poised anxiety later, a shaky voice announced itself. The boys carefully undid the lock, but not beyond the penetration of the second chain lock and a hand reached in with—the returned investment.

"Sorry for any inconvenience," the scared shitless voice intoned.

"That's all right!" uttered Hubbel.

"My girls, please."

Aaron showed them out. The party was over. Aaron and Tom wanted to leave. Aaron and Richard divided the dough in half again. Sighs. Nervous, shaking hands. The last of the bottle was passed.

Tom called a taxi. Get out of that motel room! Aaron told their griefs to the taxi driver who smiled and said, "That guy is the biggest asshole in town. If you still want women, I can get you gorgeous ones." The driver was part of the real syndicate.

"Is that for the whole night?" Tom asked.

"Are you kidding? Who can do it for the whole night? It's for fifteen minutes. Hey, Tarzan. A whole night! Ha!"

Aaron didn't want another try. Luke was still willing to put up half of Tom's fare if Aaron would. It was still eighty dollars. They left Tom in front of another motel. He met them later at the slot machines, full of praise for his own glory.

Luke exhausted himself at the tables. Later, he found himself slipping away in the tub too drained to hardly get to the bed anymore. He'd looked at all the good-looking women. One shuddered in disgust when she felt Luke's eyes rolling over her.

Confidence in the effect of the disguise was at one hundred percent. Luke awoke in his atrociously decorated room with a fierce earache. They did the worst things to him, you know.

Wentworth lurched out to find drops to ease the nerve-eating pain. Any stores open? No. He drove to the emergency room of the local hospital. Help! Patience. Hospital forms. You fill them out before being seen, though you might be hanging onto a nearly severed limb with your writing hand.

The place was full when Luke arrived. Couples who had fought were hanging onto each other. Slightly butchered lovers had to hang onto themselves. An Indian family of five was discussing how to answer the questions. A nurse with massive thighs gave Luke his forms. He tried to explain, "If I could only go to the pharmacy and get my non-prescription drops, I'd be fine. I won't have to take up vital space." A reasonable try.

The nurse heaved a sigh. This story she heard several times a shift. Luke was part of humanity now. Equalized. Sit over there (the nurse's finger pointing). There's a nice comfortable chair. Read a sportsman's magazine and think about killing us while we follow the rules. Remember. You came in. Now, suffer with the rest of us.

Luke came off as easy to push around and insult. He gave his name as Oscar Obolus. A macabre touch, even to his own mind. What made him do things like that?

There were great pictures of Alaskan brown bears shot on earth moved by a massive quake. A deer hanging flayed from a butchering post was less intriguing. A cross section diagram showed the best place to get a buck from a stationary platform. Luke read through the best way to hunt grouse, a personal experience story about facing a maddened bull elephant with only a hand gun, fishing for muskellunge on the upper Mississippi from rafts and—God! did that ear ever send torpedoes into his brain! Luke went to the desk to reiterate the case for his great, enormous, continuous and exploding hurt. The nurse looked him in the eye and said, "If you want to be seen at all, sit back down, baby."

At least fourteen people were ahead of him. And then, the worst thing. A gunshot victim was rushed in. The interns got to gather round and try their luck. It was a challenging opportunity for the young surgeons to try out what they'd been shown and see whether, they too, had the power to pull one back from the abyss.

Fortunately for Luke, whoever'd put the lead into this desperado knew how to do her work. A woman had shot the guy.

He'd wanted some forced action. She had awesome good looks, class, intellect and swagger. How else does one get close to a development like that if you, yourself, happen to be horny, hopeless, latently violent, and clumsy?

The disappointed healers were soon asking questions of the less exciting patients again. Can't pee? When was the last time you had a movement? How long have you been seeing these patterns?

Would they wake him if his turn came and he was asleep? Luke couldn't trust that. He read one magazine after another. Science, and fix-it articles. He tired dizzily to absorb the statistics. A piece about the advantage of wood burning stoves. Luke had a glimpse of L.A. festooned with smoke stacks.

It took five minutes to get the prescription for the drops. He'd even be allowed to put them in himself.

"How do I get to the pharmacy?" Once he got there, he was informed that they were out. It was ten o'clock in the morning.

"You'll be able to get them from any drugstore in town." Luke was angry, tried to show it, was completely ignored. Wait till they tried to send him a bill for his visit. Why, they'd be sending it to a dead man. Ha!

Luke bought his drops and returned to his air-conditioned room. He'd head back to L.A. that night. Why drive through the heat? Luke regretted having to sleep. It meant losing time at the tables. His regret slunk with him down into his sleep. At seven, he got up, showered, dressed, went out, wolfed a meal, bought a half-pint of Crow and drove back.

XXIX. IN WHICH LUKE FINDS OUT THAT HE, TOO, IS DEAD

Wentworth arrived at Poule's and pushed the button to gain entrance. The voice answering did not believe it was the detective returned. Someone was joking about the dead, *again*. Poule had told his entire collection of friends about the trauma he'd endured: the death of his wonderful dogs, the humiliations, the stripping of his privacy, the desecration of his property. It was probably one of Poule's business rivals at the gate trying to agitate Jack's nerves.

"Sure, Mr. Wentworth. Come right on up."

On seeing the loaned car come up the drive (a car that was never mentioned in the newspaper articles, but presumed impounded), Jack was summoned. Who was it, really? No! Not that monster again! Hadn't it been Wentworth who had directed that evil killing machine to the center of his once happy life?

Wentworth climbed out of the car, a sloppy smile on his face. Nobody seemed glad to see him. A few astounded faces. Wentworth. Returned from the dead. Smiling in a most lumpishly sinister way. A new detective was already on the job, out asking Alica's friends, the scientists and the artists questions.

And this other detective had to be paid so much more because of the dangers of the case. What was Poule going to do with two detectives?

Luke was making demands to be fed. Jack was happy to see him escorted toward the kitchen.

Now, the new man's theory was that Alica wanted to blackmail her father. Her friends were her shields. Poule told him of the murders committed and how that just couldn't be possible. The new man sulked. What a foul toilet his head was stuck down in. Poule called up and fired the guy. Wentworth had it all over him.

Luke was fed by Thelma, the woman he'd had the fight with. She didn't recognize Luke for awhile, and when she did, she poured hot coffee onto his hand. Luke leapt up from the table, but she'd already run snickering from the room. Luke wasn't hurt that badly. He even had the humor to laugh it off. Thelma hid around the edge of the kitchen door and peeped in on Luke after hearing him chuckle. They quietly forgave one another. She offered a chocolate torte in place of a peace pipe. They got into a conversation about who was dead in his place. And who was this efficiency expert who'd put the frights into old Jack?

If the torte hadn't been so delicious, (Secret recipe. In the family for seventeen generations) Wentworth would have started to worry. Faith in the disguise he wore, faith in the fact that he could now move around an inquiring ghost, gave Luke the confidence the case could still be cracked. Alica would be found. How grateful Judith might be. Luke placed her photograph prominently on his mind's bedroom wall.

Delicious Judith had heard the news of the living Luke. She caught him about to shove the last bite of torte down to the oven. She recognized him more by his appetite than his appearance. The sun-shaded, felt-hatted, super-polyester man excited her. Without saying much, she grabbed his wrist and led him to her chamber.

They had to do it with him in clothes. Luke protested that the zipper would do incredible damage to his precious one. She snapped up a pair of shears, a gleam in her eye more diabolical than any ever seen in semi-grand Inquisitioner's. She cut out the protestedly dangerous teeth with the fangs while Luke cowered, hands in trousers, willing to sacrifice fingers rather than accrue damage to his most sensory organ. ("Not true," growls Mr. Stomach.)

Remember that mirror that Luke had last seen Ms. Poule in? Well, she guided him over to it and had him behind her. She could see and he, unfortunately, was made to watch a very ugly guy manipulated. It wasn't bad, and lasted for a relatively long time.

Luke slept on Ms. Poule's bed for some hours. When he awoke, it was to her and the maid arguing outside the door. Judith was trying to get the girl to do something that violated her ethics.

"That man is a loco!"

Luke went to the door and broke up the conversation. "Can you get me another pair of pants out of my car trunk? The blue ones."

He grasped Judith by the wrist and pulled her into the room. Instead of asking questions, Luke just tried to tease it into her.

"I'm dry," Judith protested. Luke only led her to the vanity where what could pass for jelly was smeared on. What a dog! Judith half-liked the role reversal. When the maid came back, knocking on the door, Luke told her to drop the pants outside and go away. Judith tried to outshout him. She demanded she come in. Luke was hurt. The maid walked into the room using a funereal step. It soon became "heigh-ho the dare-ee-oh!" for three. There was revulsion and disgust on both sides. Ultimately, to Judith's delight, that intensified the conflict. She was the center of the struggle. Luke doubled-up in laughter when the maid's tongue finally achieved its target, only to be repelled by a taste as unpalatable as ink.

This time, when the shears were found, Wentworth did not stay to talk to them. He sped towards the door with the uncut pair of pants in hand.

The maid, although naked, did not leave off the chase. Luke tripped her as she came around the corner screaming about she was going to do to Luke. He grabbed the shears as she went down against the pedestal of a Mezzo-American art piece. A woman giving birth, I think. The figure shook in its plexiglass case, almost falling, but the frightened maid's hands steadied it. If that crashed, goodbye pay for twenty years. Better disappear into Central America yourself. When she looked around, Wentworth had exited. She went back to Judith's room where the mistress was waiting, cleaned-off, and they explored other climes from there.

Luke hurried to find Poule and find out what state his Jenny was in.

Jenny had "moved out." Sam would give Luke the details. Poule said that he was happy to see Luke back on the case. He gave him two days to find his daughter. After that, Poule said that he was going to turn to other methods. Poule placed a lot of money into Luke's hand and a bonus was promised for a find. Poule was bluffing, but thought Luke worked better (as demonstrated) under pressure. Actually, Poule had paid to have Jenny "fall in love." He couldn't stand to have the waif's pimply face and wedgie eyes staring at him during meals.

Sam, discarded lover, mumbled a few softly embarrassed excuses and provided Luke with a Poule Enterprises business card. One of the faithful's. The address underlined.

Luke confidently zipped up his fly before placing himself behind the wheel to motor over to the location. Jenny was staying at 1543 Elusive, a street nervously close to Apollo Drive up in the Canyon.

Wentworth was greeted by his daughter at the front door. He briefly had to endure remaining unrecognized and treated like an unwanted door-to-door gadget salesman. There followed a brief reconciliation and promises of fidelity and happiness. Yeah, sure.

"Oh, daddy! I'm so glad you're alive—ha, ha, but how funny you look! I wouldn't have recognized it was you in a zillion years!"

"We don't have a zillion years. The sun's already exhausted half its fuel."

Luke was led around to the rear of the house where Jenny had been sunning in a chaise. A superior expression appeared on her clearing face's nastily lurid lips. Jenny had a supply of canned mixed drinks. Daiquiris mostly, but there were a few cans of tequila sunrise and whisky sours left. Dad refused the bait and demanded to hear her story.

Jenny sniped that she was waiting for "Janet" to return from work. Luke had already put it together. He jerked Jenny over his knee, exposed her bottom and imposed his hand of authority over the, ugh, pimply, surface of it. Jenny wasn't passive. Her fingernails tried to grope into daddy's side. Luke kept having to slap the bitten to the quick nails aside.

Luke flopped his daughter off into the pool. Coming up, Jenny began to holler abuses. It was plain truth to Luke. He had lost control. He gave his daughter up to the waves. Almost, anyway. When Jenny tried to climb out, he shoved her back in a couple of times. That raised her fury a bit closer to frenzy. He could hear crying and her feet running. A heavy object or a sharp one was probably in her hands. He stepped out of the front door and crossed the tiny yard to get back to his car. On the way, he passed "Janet." No prizes. This was how Poule handled everything. Poor Jenny! Wait till she found out that she was to be adored only for the duration of the case.

XXX. IN WHICH IT IS EXPLORED WHETHER IT'S FEAR THAT MAKES US SMART

L uke was all for declaring himself to his enemies. But where were they? His misadventures thus far make a stupid story. Flat characters take the place of possible developments in character, plot and setting. It's completely over-manipulated. Luke's head is only a hollowed out squash. Laughs. What for?

Luke he tried to strangle his present mood. He felt real pain! Anguish. Character is destiny! And if you have none? Rejection. Luke suddenly looked into himself and saw the eyes of all of Poule's women, minus Alica's. He squeezed the steering wheel wanting it to absorb his hostility and unadulterated anger. Life was exciting him a bit too much these days.

Luke stopped at a phone booth and got Boil's address. "Never bug a bugger," Wentworth's Kant professor used to say. (Like a shot off a shovel). Luke smelled his breath. Stinking of dirty ways, he was reminded of the great thinker's alcoholic obsession for small boys or anyone who still carried the look.

Those hands had tried to go after him! No thanks. The Cappadocian clap snapped a photo of his earthly daze. Luke needed to figure a way of shaking down Boil without losing his disguise. Luke felt the void sizing him up. It's always ready to suck you back into the blackness of darkness. That's enough. A fresh plan came to the sleuth.

Luke directed his gray car to an enormous clothing discount house. He purchased workman's black-green overalls. They fit completely over his polyesters. A pair of rubbers to slide over the white shoes. A ski mask that exposed no more than the mouth and tip of the nose. And a tool box.

Boil's abode was on Druid Street, not far from the campus. A have-the-students-over for lunch kind of residence. An adobe framed palms. Luke drove past several times before choosing a spot to park, later that night. Luke reached into the glove compartment and reacquainted himself with the gun. There wouldn't be any easily jimmied or opened sliding doors this time. Luke decided to rape the lock and other approaches to Boil. But, in the meanwhile, Mr. Stomach told Luke what to do.

Luke picked his favorite, hole-in-the-wall Thai restaurant. Looking as he did, the maître d's wondered whether the tourist was lost. Did he have any idea of what he was in for? Our Thai food is hot. "Very hot," the waiter tried to tell the still sunglass-bespeckled gentleman in the baggy blue polyester pants with matchingly insane shirt divided by the white belt. They just never got customers like this.

Luke was pleased that his pal Miki couldn't see into him. He was escorted to a table near the toilet in case the food went through him too fast. But the guest asked to be seated at the one Luke Wentworth always wanted, the one facing an ornate screen whose colors and figures danced for you if you ate and drank right.

A Thai meal is based on rice. The number and variety of dishes available is, however, only limited by the cook's imagination and patience, and the restaurant's and the client's budgets. All of which were near supreme at this place. The only cut rate touch was that the beautiful girls in costume didn't perform traditional numbers while you ate and the music was bitterly repetitious. It's customary to have a soup, two or more Kaengs (dishes with gravy) and as many side dishes as Mr. S. demands.

Luke surprised his observers by knowing these things and not needing the basic tour of the menu that most lost-looking customers asked for.

Without dithering, Luke ordered that Kung-Tom Yam, the office clerk at headquarters (prawn soup), Kaeng Chad Mu Kai, the minister of fine skies (pork and chicken soup), Mu Wan, and Kai Tod Tauches, the Siamese twins in charge of agriculture and defense (sweet pork and deep fried chicken with yellow bean sauce), be brought before him.

Wasn't there something familiar about that voice and manner? The stranger even ate the dishes (and he ordered more!) with his fingers—the traditional Thai way of eating that makes the food taste even better, especially when the sauces mingle on the fingers.

The guest asked if any Lag Chap was available for desert (small magic-tiny molded fruits made of mung bean pastes, sweetened with sugar and colored with fresh fruits and vegetables (but here, alas, with artificial substitutes). Who is the only person who asks for that dish every time on the off chance that it could be had? (There was once some leftover after a wedding and Luke had gotten some and, ever since then ….

"Mr. Wentworth!"

But this was not Luke Wentworth! How could it be?

"Mr. Wentworth?"

"Miki?"

"Why, sir, what has happened to you?"

"It's too long a tale to tell, Miki. Have you got any Fat Horses back there?"

"We have Galloping Horses, Mr. Wentworth."

"No, just some Pratad Loin."

How had Luke stumbled upon this heaven? One night, after he had to I.D. a friend at the morgue. He'd shot himself in a mall (at Christmas near the reindeer) because his wife was leaving him (broke). Luke had stumbled in full of bile against silly suicides and marriage.

The wall figures were moving for Luke. He'd had a lot of saké and Kirin to help him steam towards a solution as to how to terrorize Boil.

Luke drove to a hotel somewhere between the campus and Boil's home. But first, he needed a rest. He turned a corner and was on a street lined with fast food joints and motels. At the first place he stopped, Luke read the sign welcoming the folks to town for the "Surviving Death" seminar sponsored by the university theological department and underwritten by the Mortician's Unions of North and South America. Upon seeing a couple with what looked like a stuffed relative held between approach the desk, Wentworth turned round and walked rapidly back to his car.

At the next motel, a small sign on the reception desk advertised "Snappy." The desk clerk's very large piranha needed a bigger home. This place's rates were equal to the others' but there was no free T.V. OK. It was clean of near corpses and that's all Wentwart wanted for the moment.

In olden times, narcotics would not still the tooth that nibbled at the soul. But now's now and Luke was soon asleep.

His wake-up call was 3 a.m.

It was a rotten nightmare. He couldn't find anyone willing to take it out. A busy invisible weaver that refused to pause was stitching a pattern from Wentworth's nerve endings. Whose little place setting would the final product's be? Why wouldn't the weaver take even a five minute coffee break? He tried to ask the weaver, but Luke did not have an x-ray voice. He was separated from it by a wall of lead. Luke only wanted to be able to say a few words to the tireless toiler. The (bee-like) shuttle (from flower to hive to dance the news of the new find) refused to stop. Figures uncoiled from the loom and formed themselves into computer readouts of what man's deaf destiny was to be. Finally, Luke found a door that opened to a room where the weaver was working. The loom exhaled a penetrating sigh. Luke slammed the door to free himself from whose sound it was—all the dead. Is your time your own?

Wentworth's dream kept permutating randomly. Was the universe inside-out or outside-in? What white/black unintelligent power generated it? Here we are, diverted from comprehension and only flickering through. Even in dream, Wentworth was no alchemist. The distillation of essence that offered itself to him was handled like $10 by a drunk. But he had it given to him anyway—how to make Boil crawl.

XXXI. PAGES OF VIOLENCE, TERROR, AND EASYGOING INJUSTICE

There was a party going down the street from where Wentworth wanted to park. He had to drive around the block several times before he found a spot, not too far away from the target. It was sufficiently shaded and dark, allowed him to put the working togs and rubbers on over his clothes. The only last thing to hope was that Ali Boilba was sleeping alone.

Luke used a previously unmentionable article—a glasscutter —to make his way into the basement of the house. Using a flashlight (believe me, all this stuff was in the tool box Luke had bought, along with tape to plaster shut any loud mouths and "other" criminally intelligent things), Luke found a light switch. Now, up those stairs.

Hell, there was a lock on the cellar door! Luke had more trouble crawling out than in getting down in. What next? The mind was tensing a bit. Luke walked away from the house, around to the side. An air-conditioner was making lakefuls of noise and took up the only window. Around the back, Luke would have had better luck if a figure next door hadn't come out onto the enclosed porch area. She threw on the light, sat in a lounge chair and began pouring vodka into a glass of milk. She ate cookies and stared straight ahead at the painted purple-black back fence.

Luke hated to, but he walked out in front of the house to the other side. The good side, as it turned out. Luke carefully operated on the screen. Only got one metal splinter in his thumb as he slid into the house.

Putting the tool box on the floor, he fumbled for the flashlight and tumbled its beam around the room.

Luke almost let out a scream that would have raised a deaf mute to attention. The room glittered with sparkling eyes. Behind him, to the side of him, in front of him. He would have thought below and above him if it hadn't rapidly figured out he was in a trophy room. A black bear holding a fishing hat bedecked with trout flies in its paws was the proudest prize. For the rest, it was antelope, deer and moose. A jaguar, illegally hunted, was above Boil's bed. (It had scarred one of the guides pretty badly and was about Boil's best story outside of some hysterical "adventures in the profession" kind he eloquently specialized in). But Luke never got to see it.

There were definitely guns in the house. Luke went on hoping that they were all in the case he was having a look at. No pistols, only hunting rifles. Luke calculated that Boil would have a private weapon around somewhere. He tried opening Boil's den/study desk drawer. Again, locked. Luke put on the ski mask, figuring that he was safe, and began turning on the lights that lead up the stairs to Boil's bedroom.

Luke walked up to the former team researcher's bed and nuzzled the barrel of the silencer against Boil's ear. Reflex was to lift an arm from under the sheets and swat away the pesky midge, mosquito, or other winged misery. Boil bolted up as if lightning struck when his fingertips felt the black metal cylinder. He met his night crawling oppressor's gun, now forced tightly under the chin.

"Up! Levez vous! Arise!"

"What do you want?" Boil snapped. "And who are you? A burglar? A renegade?"

"Up, Chunky. Down the stairs."

Luke had never meant Obolus any physical harm. Luke could tell the man was soft. Here he had a snapping turtle pulled out of the bottom mud of his native pond. The jaws were monstrous and the shell hard. Wentworth was nastier a bit. Three tones past before. No cats first. Deal directly with the flesh. Make the mind scream through the irrational fields.

Boil had on a pair of light striped cotton pajamas. Luke made Aloysius abandon them. Wentworth put a braided throw rug in front of the stove and placed a kitchen chair in its center while holding the gun to Boil's ear. The President of the Journal Club was asked to sit. Boil snickered at the thief's outfit. Luke heard, became amused himself, decided to play his role with a gruff tremor in his voice. "Where's the stocks, securities, and cash stashed?"

Before able to volunteer an insured answer, Aloysius found his mouth taped shut. He tried to get up from the chair, but was shoved by a stronger hand down.

Luke hummed, "There's a Yellow Rose of Texas that I am bound to see…," as he taped Boil to the chair. "This is naturally going to hurt like hell upon rescue. Relative to how long it takes to find you, of course." Luke interrupted the sixth bar to inform Boil, "But that's what it's all about—the pain we suffer as we hibbly-hobbly through life."

Boil was beginning to sweat. His eyes lost confidence and began to stare frighteningly at the ridiculous figure relaxing in a chair opposite, smoking through a hole in the ski mask. No hurry. Suspend time. Manipulate the politely silent observer's apprehensive desire to have a positive fix, smell out behavioral clues. Even false ones. Something to be able to survive what might be coming next.

"Nice kitchen. Makes you feel comfortable right away. "And the trophies, in there," Luke pointing, "what a shot you must be! What a dangerous man." Luke left his seat and came over to pat and squeeze Aloysius' cheek. Boil tried to wriggle away, tried making noise by thumping the chair on the floor. Between the rug and the air-conditioner, hardly a thundercrack. Still, Boil got a nicely vicious slap across the chops.

Luke started some hot water on and searched the cabinets for tea or coffee. Coffee. Boil preferred using a drip grind, a Mellita. After setting the filter and other stuff up for use, Luke slid off to use the bathroom.

Wentworth slipped off the mask and had a look at himself. He was going to let it grow back in on top. Pretty soon, he could be himself again. Putting a hand in front of his mouth, he tested his breath. Definitely putrid. He used Boil's toothbrush, and then mouthwashed the pesthole out. During his stay in the john, Luke's eyes spied Boil's razor and shaving cream. Putting his mask back on, he took these back to the kitchen. He knew Boil was anxiously thinking, What's he doing? What's next! Sizing the assailant up. Was he a foreign op? FBI? Private? What?

Luke re-entered. Boil feverishly twisted his neck to see. The shaving kit, placed next to the coffee. Boil got ready for humiliation. He told himself, Toughen-up. A tactic like that, shaving your head, groin or whatever, isn't going to turn you into a flowing fountain of information.

Luke drank some coffee, walked round the room, looked at wall hangings, potted plants, fingered woodwork, killed time. The refrigerator was his last stop. Luke lingered in its opened light for quite awhile in contemplation of its contents. He reached a hand in and pulled out a half-eaten marble cake. He lifted his mask up under his nose and chomped away behind Boil's back.

After doing all of these things, Luke presented himself before the chairman of several powerful university board committees in a half crouch. He stared directly into Boil's angry and solid eyes. Boil had decided the intruder wasn't dangerous, or was waiting for someone else to arrive.

"Looks to me like you're not afraid of a shave number. No, you're looking, under the circumstances, composed. Well, I have to follow orders anyway. And, since you're not going to mind, I guess it'll be alright. It'll save me having to explain later. They wear me out. I've never been patient. Ever."

So Luke went ahead and shaved off all of Boil's exposed hair. The tape was going to leave patches and stripes. Wentworth nicked his man in several places and blood trickled in tiny streams over Boil's body. Luke affected the posture of a sculptor and moved back to size up the work. He returned to the marble cake owner and nicked him three or four more places. Wentworth began to orate on, "The importance of meaning in everyday life," and how, "The public will never be safe."

After a few more purposeful nicks, (as opposed to ones Boil presumed accidental), Boil felt the inkling that he was not dealing with anyone representing anyone. Just look at that outfit again! This guy was nuts. He was doomed to be maimed and butchered by a freak!!! All Boil's working was going to be destroyed by a joyriding psychotic!!! Oh, no! Boil's defenses were useless! This guy didn't want to know anything. HYe just wanted to see pain, blood and hurt. Boil began to cry.

"Oh, what's the matter? The master know now that they'll be no more sunrises for him?" Wentworth too the kettle of boiling water off the stove, let out a scraking cackle (he'd warmed to the role) and dripped the water on Boil's feet. The body writhed, and twitched and needed to scream. The chair hammer-tapped the rug arhythmically.

"It's a whole new world. Silent, isn't it? Africa. Ordering the execution squad to line up. Remember how you liked barking those commands? The soldiers so spit-sharp going through the manual of arms and snapping rifle butts into their shoulders, awaiting your order to fire. Snap 'em back into the belly of their tribal maker! Or—there's your mistress walking arm in arm down a Spanish colonial street. Four hundred years ago. He owns so many more Indians than you and has them working the mines."

The psychopath left off raving and walked back and forth in front of poor Boil who was now convinced that the razor in the madman's waving hand was going to end up tracing a line across his throat. He'd bleed to death like the pigs in the slaughterhouse he worked for summers as an undergraduate. This butcher's eyes were like those of the lifers' in the meat packing plant. They'd been killing for so long that a detour into human flesh wouldn't bother them a nanosecond.

Luke had repositioned himself in the benevolent glow of the open refrigerator door. The freezer was attacked. Luke dropped what he didn't want. Ka-thud. Pork. Roast, veal, trout. Ka-thud, ka-thud, ka-thud. Finally, he restationed himself in front of the, evidently, near convulsive Ph.D. with half a popsicle in hand. Boil stared wildly. But….

Luke finished the popsicle and threw the stick over his shoulder. "Now I'm a housewife! Just look at me. All in a dither because I've had to be away for the weekend and couldn't water my houseplants. None of my neighbors likes me. They think I'm strange. Imagine that. They refuse to take care of them. And here you are, my favorite, half animal, half plant, favorite darling. I'll water you first!" Wentworth poured a stream of the hot stuff down Boil's spinal column.

Aloysius shuddered. His bowels eviscerated in uneven spasms. Boil's nostrils got the message. Now he smelled like the animals in the plant. He gave up hope. All the faces of possible rescuers on his mental merry-go-round stopped appearing in the corner of the room. Boil was in shock and about to pass out when he was doused (Oh, scream murder! Baby, please!!) with a bowl of cold water.

"OK, fun's over, Professor Boil."

His name, he heard his name! It was only a shakedown for information. He was saved!

"Where's Alica Poule?" Luke ripped the tape off Boil's mouth, but kept it ready to paste back on.

"Whhennnwoorthhh? But—you're dead! Yoooouuuu'rrreee dead."

"You're the one who's almost dead, asshole. You've got one chance to tell me where Poule's daughter is or it's your dick."

"She's left me," Boil whimpered.

"Where's to. That's all I want to hear. You think I make a habit of listening to other people's sorrows, Boil?"

Aloysius drooled slightly. On himself, so Wentworth didn't mind. "You scared me shitless in that outfit. I thought you were...."

Luke free hand carried over with more boiling liquid. Boil opened for a scream, but Wentworth closed him up before Ali could let it go.

"Last few words I have to say to you professor. I don't care what you guys are up to. Sorry about your pal. I'm going to open you up just one more time. When I do, it's to hear a name and address. Anything else, I burn it. Even if I do, you're not out of the woods. You could die of shock, rotting in this kitchen a couple of days unless I make a call, say to Dranthus, tonight. I know you don't want the police. Be a good fellow. Tell all, in as few words as possible."

Luke opened. Boil told. He started to plead for the phone call. Luke sealed the cavern. "I get the girl, you get the call." Boil looked up frenzied. More betrayal! He wanted to put Wentworth's head in the trophy den. We don't know our limits. Boil needed to bank on luck to survive. Alica was out of town and wasn't that easily reached. The cocksucker had lied! Lied! Lied!

Luke took off his costume in the foyer, folded it neatly under his arm, and locked the front door behind him.

XXXII. IN WHICH THE TIGHT HOLE OF LUCK CONTINUES TO DEFY LUKE

Wentworth was tired. Exhausting work, torture. Luke felt only slightly satisfied, but glad he was holding a good hand. Other players still in the game. Can't risk certainty. Can't risk that all the little forces out there wouldn't conspire to throw a wrench at your swelled head.

The water wasn't nearly as muddy now. If the sun came up at dawn, instead of waiting for the smog to clear, it would be with Wentworth as he walked back to his car. It was. You could even see the snow on the mountains. Damn! And a rainbow, too! An insomniac sitting on his porch said, "Hello," to Luke as he passed. Luke was friendly in return. He passed several people out with their dogs. On leashes. Small, so small. No panic.

On the second floor of a duplex, he could see a young girl silhouetted on her windowshade having trouble with the snaps of her bra. "Still half asleep," Luke whispered as he continued on.

Six houses before he got to his car, a boy on a big-wheel

raced out of a driveway in front of Luke and stopped. The bird-boned boy shot Wentworth a hateful before furiously peddling down the block, until, trying to take the corner, he wiped out.

All the coffee Mr. Wentworth drank while conversing with Professor Boil was making Luke freaky. He didn't want to stay in the same area, so he headed across town, taking ganders at what was still fresh at this hour. Nothing. Street cleaners. Night desperadoes. The city gets tired, but never manages a therapeutic rest. Everyone should be marched up into the hills for a day or two every year.

Driving Wilshire at this hour always reminded him of his visits to the city morgue at similar hours on unrecallable days. The one would join the rest. No one needed its fingerprints. Let things happen as they will, the police and national guard will serve you when the summers get too hot. No matter how much ammunition you store, they have more.

Tell them about the time you hunted down the blue-eyed movie star. Luke, don't be humble. The time you and Packard smashed that bunch of pseudo-psychedelic religious fanatics who worked under the guide of a self-proclaimed messiah born in Hindustan. He couldn't speak English, but knew to amass his loose millions to invest in Microsoft. You should have followed his lead. Luke can't speak. He's a dummy, a galley slave plowing through the blue Mediterranean under the lash of a tyrant who's going to unshackle him to fight Typhoeus on behalf of Zeus. You're holding deuces, Wentworth. Drop your oar and hope for better luck in the next life. Luke, stop talking to yourself.

Stop! Ah, what's the use? We fool ourselves with the stories we tell ourselves, about how it all must be. It's all wrong.

Here's Luke pounding on Eagan's door. Hans is tying the ends of his bathrobe, doesn't recognize his pal since he's dead and he doesn't get up to answer the door for dead men.

"Sure you're at the right address, Bud?"

"Just let me have your couch, you lustful jerk-off."

Hans didn't ever shock. He may have blinked once. Eagan ushered Luke, hand stretched out, into the innards of his home. Eagan sat by his crashed friend to hear a story, but Luke fell immediately into the following second-string dream.

A man without teeth in a purple dyed hair shirt was trying to put his fingers into Luke's pocket. Luke cuffed him one on the side of the head. The man turned into a saber-toothed tiger. (Wentworth had maybe cruised by the La Brea Tar Pits on his voyage from Boil's kitchen over to Eagan's). Luke turned chicken and raced away. The gigantic cat did not follow. When he looked back, there was Boil, hairless and standing at attention. Luke wanted to know why Boil was there. As he turned to go back and ask, Boil became the saber-tooth and Luke balked again.

Wentworth was the last man alive on a packet steamer crossing the North Atlantic. He could see passengers and shipmates floating face downwards close to the sinking ship. He climbed what there was left of a mast and waited for the water. Something was nibbling at his leg. He tried to shake it off and awoke to face Eagan who told him to either stop screaming or find another haven.

When Luke rolled over this time, he was out of the ocean. Where was he? In deep space, one of a crew of four scientists commanding an outpost station mostly manned by somatic androids out to take photos of even more distant universes. The work was (very naturally) boring and the four humans hated each another. Lisa was forever taking the droids apart to see how close she could come to making them experience "human" pain. Stanley liked to have the droids fool around with him. Massages better than any offered at Poule's. Other services were administered throughout the pleasure predicant's off-duty time.

Wentworth was dedicated to his work. He chased phenomenon even when he wasn't officially logged in. The least probabilistic of the crew, he was interested in mapping everything observable and doing extensive work cataloging the spectrum analysis of every charted body. On his last round of duty, he had been privileged to witness a supernova. The other members of the crew didn't even bother to come see when called. Wentworth let the androids serve him coffee, draw his bath, clean uniforms, serve food and the like, but he never let them distract him from his work.

Andy never left his compartment except to do duty time. He once saw a comet pass without ever thinking to call Wentworth. The other two, Luke tolerated well enough, but Andy, what a fatigued caricature, uninterested in the unfolding charms of ever-deepening and developing Truth. He was … Why, all he did was sleep his off-duty time away. He wouldn't show up on new century days to celebrate with the others. Andy made about the same use for the droids as Luke. The imitation of his habits annoyed him. Andy even had the gall to borrow Luke's programs for the desired droid routines.

Wentworth loved space. The satisfactions were innumerable. Something new always happening. "Oh, please, never let me leave this dream," Wentworth begged. The mid-afternoon sun slipped through a missing chink in the blinds and gouged Luke's eyes.

Went dragged himself off the couch and threw himself (after unclothing) into the shower. Eagan's voice could be heard between pants from the bedroom yelling to Luke not to use all of the hot water. Don't worry, Hans. Our boy's taking his cold. Goose pimples. Luke had been perspiring heavily on the couch. The shower brought him to full alert, awareness of his massive hunger.

Wentworth was startled by warm fingers placed on his shoulders. Turning off the faucets, he banged him against the frame of the metal door. Besty laughed at his changed appearance. Hans told her where she could find the joke and she'd hurried over to see it. All she wore was a pair of Eagan's boxer shorts. Besty wondered what was up with Luke. He was supposed to be jealous and excited. The changes he'd gone through must be mental as well as physical. The two reflect infinitely on one another, don't you think?

"How's Ahmed?"

"Gone to Moslem paradise to walk in gardens and be served by ever faithful women."

Hans Otto came in to announce a plan for lunch. Luke had to decline the invitation to satisfy his stomach's foodlust.

"Are you sure? It's first class Syrian," said Otto polishing the hook.

"Yes. I've got a bead on the maiden. Got to get to her. Now." He didn't want to hang with Hans and Betsy.

"Pity." Hans threw an arm around Betsy's shoulders and played sincere. Downcast eyes. "Do you want some real clothes or are you still Parzival?"

"Safer to fool around for awhile longer."

"Poor boy. Shoot to kill if you have to," Bets advised.

"Always."

She stopped taking him for a squeamish toe shooter. Hans saw her realize Luke was no slacker at killing time and got her away.

Luke in front of the mirror. He brushed his teeth and popped aspirin. The top of the head was evidencing stubble. By tonight, it'd be over. He could hear Eagan trying to calm the Bestsy down in the bedroom. Hans on the crusade to Syria alone? Luke heard the front door slam. Eagan came in sore.

"What'd you have to hint at something like that for?"

"Well, she was hinting she had the boyfriend killed."

"She was only bluffing and you know it."

"Sure?"

"Well, of course. Ahmed owns the restaurant we were going to."

"Why was she so hot to hurt him then?"

"One night Ahmed got carried away and gave her a bad case of vaginitis."

"That all?"

"He ripped her open so bad she had to have stitches."

"Mad about the humiliation?"

"Yeah. Listen, bud, no more about what you've done with a gun in your day in the presence of ladies, OK? Save it for the poker party suckers. Deal?"

"Sure. Look, I'm sorry. She came on like she was hard stuff."

"The usual big-screen filtered wide-angle shot, friend. The close-ups reveal all the tiny thousands of nasty little lines. Thought you knew a doomed woman when you smelled one? Pressure slowing you down?"

"Yup." Wentworth leaned forward with his hands sliding up the thighs of the sink until only his eyes and forehead were still in the mirror, "Not much longer. Go to Ensenada soon."

Eagan was placated and left to make a call. Wentworth suited up and wheeled to Rutt's Inn, a Westside transplanted Hawaiian breakfast and lunch place. He was thinking, "Teritaco" when one of the rear tires went "*sssssssss*" and flat. He hobbled to a gas station. Two miles. Too bent to try any jack work.

When he got to the service station, the guy said that he could have it done in three quarters of an hour. Fully scheduled for the afternoon, but changing a tire could be worked in. Luke made his way to a bar rather than wait around the station. Three or four Cokes and a lousy sandwich later, he went to pick up his car. From a block away he could see it still jacked up outside one of the garage doors. He should have stayed to coach things along. Wentworth could feel it beginning to rain wrenches.

The tire couldn't be changed because there was no spare. You mean to tell me that Luke had never noticed whether or not there was a spare tire in all this time? Sure, why not?

The service station attendant explained that the old tire couldn't be patched. He produced a four inch nail and showed Luke the odd angle it had punctured the rubber, making a patch impossible. Would Luke like to buy a new tire? Special sale on. He was lucky. But, aw, wouldn't you know it—out of the particularly odd-sized imported tire that was on the car. So on two new matching tires. He was getting quite a savings at the present price. Did he know that?

Luke never abandoned his frown during the ordeal. Ill omens began to appear in the sky. The traffic helicopter was overhead. Luke pulled up in front of a liquor store and bought a half-pint of Crow. He remembered the memory of the first live baseball game he'd ever seen. The cub scouts got to go down to Fenway to see the Red Sox beat the White Sox in one of the only games the Red won that month. Luke remembered the two alcoholics who had sat behind the troop taking slugs from pints tucked in rumpled paper bags. Occasionally, the label peered out above the top of a trembling bag. One drunk kept pointing curious Luke forward. "Was he an idiot? Ted Williams was at bat. Watch the game!" Luke missed Ted's solo homer over the left field wall.

We find a little of everything in our memory. It's maybe a kind of pharmacy/chem lab in which chance guides the hand—now to a calming drug, next to a dangerous poison. So why reach if it's dependent on chance and you can't read any of the labels in the dark? Luke needed something to dissipate the superstition building out of the flat tire. Bad luck coming in threes. Odd sizes. Time lost. Felt like a hair stuck across your cheek you can't see or find with your fingertips. You keep brushing at it because it's irritating. Existence sits serenely composed, a sea anemone, sealed on the organism that's become its prey.

Behind his wheel and simultaneously back at the stadium, the stubble-faced drunk's hoary finger pointing forward. Luke, revolted by the realization that two or three simple burned-in images so easily manipulated mood, mind, action, and character. What was Luke's history after all? Facts that were becoming lies. Luke took a few more hits from the bottle and pulled the rear view mirror onto himself. Travelling at high speed, slashing his way to the finish of a case that, from the moment he'd accepted, he'd handled it wrongly. Another slug, a few more. He'd soon be facing Ms. Poule and totaling up the deaths, drinks, lays and trouble. He didn't want to be too sober when he caught up to her. If the broken, rescued, and illuminated, disillusioned rewarded and humbled cycle would only hurry to end. "Money makes iron float," was the only conviction that Wentworth retained belief in. The time for that had its endings hinted at, too.

He felt the terror that was in him like the time he and a date fell off the huge orange raft shooting the whitewater on the Colorado. She'd gotten off with a few scrapes. He'd been dragged across the rocks and bruised his ribs. He'd gone under, grazed his head, had it occur to him that he'd never be coming up.

Whoa! Slipped off into his cups. Not quite over the line. There are several thousand reflex circuits in the human body, automatic and unthinking. They keep the organism alive and healthy but, so what. Here comes a cop. Luke, you really shouldn't drive 75 mph. While Wentworth's being stopped and dodges losing his license, let's have a look at how Boil is doing. He may yet get to make his mark on the outcome of the document of this electrochemical adventure.

XXXIII. IN WHICH BOIL SAYS ENOUGH TO CHANGE WHAT SHOULD HAVE HAPPENED

Boil had to keep smelling himself and not kowtow to the pain waves from his second-degree burns. While tied to that chair, with the rather too stark kitchen light trying to tear his eyes out every time he regained consciousness (head thrown back staring directly into it), Boil was full of hate. Shaw says "Hatred is the coward's revenge for being intimidated." But that's not completely right here. Boil was undone with a great deal of the weight from his intimidator's hands. Hoffer says, "Passionate hatred can give meaning to and purpose to an empty life." But, although Boil's gotten to passionate hatred, he doesn't need it for purpose. Nietzsche wrote, "There is a jealousy in hating too, we want to have our enemy for ourselves." Ah, yes. No! De Fontenelle, in writing about happiness says, "You can tell a happy man by the sort of immobility of his situation." If we change happiness to hatred in this clause, we'd be closer to Boil's feelings.

At about the time Luke was waking on Eagan's couch, Boil's

good friend Dr. Mark Tropp came by to see if there'd been any new "wrinkles" in the affair. Alica had dumped Boil. As a friend, Tropp thought it his duty to pry and persecute Boil as much as possible. He wanted to help expurgate the pain. Tropp found its viewing excellent fun.

Tropp had tried to call Boil at his office. The departmental secretary had said that the professor hadn't been in, that he was probably tied up elsewhere or in committee. Mark drove from his office directly to Boil's home. Aloysius was infrequently anywhere else.

Tropp found no answer to his doorbell ringing. But Boil might be "occupied" or playing a game. Tropp felt very much in the inferior position when dealing with Boil. Boil was such the trickster. "There was no rush to be rushed," Tropp told himself. He took a stroll alongside the house to see if Boil might be working in the back. As he passed by the den, looking heavenwards and neighborwards mostly, he tripped over the screen that blended in so nicely with the unmown lawn. It took him awhile to see where the screen had come from. It had not been created by spontaneous generation and its edges even looked clipped.

Dr. T. tried to pull himself up to see through the window. Couldn't do it. Saw a light shining from under the den door. Very strange. The doctor looked around for something he could stand on to help him. The garage was a tomb. Only the body of the car. Finally, Tropp decided that there was no more time to waste. He pulled out his cellular phone and called for help.

Dranthus must come right over. "I've got a class to teach in fifteen minutes. Can't it wait?"

"Aloysius may be lying murdered in his home. It's definitely been at least burglarized. What else it may be, God knows! We have to get inside and find out."

"Be right over."

Tropp searched for something for Dranthus to stand on.

Boil's mind was running over his beliefs, separating the firm from culturally implanted. "The real and legitimate goal of the sciences is the endowment of human life with ... And no senseless dick should have ever even had the opportunity to accidentally stop ... Suffering, this ... The sole origin of consciousness ... If science could operate unchecked, a world state and no more ... Not true that every kind of organization dulls humanity ... I stink, I'm a stirred stink. Arraggghh! I'm a mess. Won't they please hurry up and find me? Oh, Mummy, it hurts!

Dranthus hopped up and through the window. No trouble except for some wire slivers into the tips of his fingers when he grabbed the sill to go through. He found Boil messy and distasteful. What kind of lunatic had been in there with him? Shaved, tied with adhesive, cut all over with a razor, burned, beaten ... Dranthus was glad to see that at least Aloysius was passed out and not consciously suffering. He let the doctor in and together they tried to remove the tape without hurting. But they were unsuccessful. Boil screamed so loudly that they had to re-tape his mouth shut.

The doctor wrote out a few prescriptions and sent Edgar out to get them filled. Boil was laid face down on another throw rug, the Persian, brought in from the study. Dranthus took the filthy one and dumped it in the garbage on his way out.

Dr. Tropp made a phone call and arranged a room in a private hospital. He didn't like the crazed-animal look gushing from Boil's eyes. His patient was dehydrated, but Tropp was afraid of giving him drink until the pain could be sedated.

Dranthus returned with ointment and narcotics. After the injections, Dranthus was all for asking questions. The doctor objected, saying that it was necessary to get Boil into the hospital as quickly as possible so that tests could be run. "Do you want his brain damaged? He's in shock and could collapse into a coma. Die from having protracted pneumonia sitting naked in this air-conditioning."

"OK, OK."

"He's not dead, the clever little devil," Boil mumbled as Dranthus and Tropp argued. But neither heard that. "Heap not debt, da clebber litter debble." They passed it over as raving.

"How long before he can talk, Tropp?"

"We'll get something out of him by late this afternoon, early tonight."

"Will that be soon enough?"

"All this," said Tropp pointing a finger around the room at the wreckage, defrosted meat on the floor, "smacks more of lunacy than of methodical interrogation."

"On the surface it does," retorted Dranthus viciously. "Oh, you think…," said Tropp putting a finger to his lips thoughtfully.

"Sure, why not?"

"But a few drugs in the arm and they would have known all in as long as it took to tell."

"Who's to say that wasn't done? The rest might all be theater to stall our suspicions."

"Then by all means, let's speed to the hospital and see what's flowing through his veins."

"I'll drive the car around back."

"Help me dress him first!"

Getting Boil into some clothes took some doing. They looked around for a hat to hide the head's scars. Finally had to take the fishing cap away from the bear for Boil.

They tucked him into the back seat and placed a blanket over him.

"Is that a Royal Coachman?" Tropp pointed at one of the flies.

"No, that's only a regular coachman."

"Are you sure?"

"Drive the car, you idiot! I don't know one fly from another. Do I look like I fish to you?"

"You can't tell just by looking." Tropp said as he backed out of the driveway and into an oncoming car.

Boil sat bolt upright upon impact and demanded that the committee adjourn if no one had any useful proposals to submit.

"Give him one of these. And, for heaven's sake, get him back down! I'll go talk to the driver of the other vehicle."

Dranthus glared at Tropp. "Hurry it up."

"Not much damage on either side," said Tropp resumption of his position behind the wheel. Dranthus pouted. No words were exchanged on the way to the cache.

Luke got a small ticket and a big scolding. The officer had an exercise grip attached to his holster to build up his muscles. The computer would want to know why a dead man had been given a summons in a very short while. At the very least, this hinted at an even more complicated murder than was presently being investigated. Luke hoped that Jenny hadn't called Ingrid to rat that the ghost who squawks still was. Nah. They wouldn't be talking to one another. Would they?

Wentworth arrived. Blythe Avenue, four blocks southwest, behind Rancho Park. He knocked half-hopefully expecting to see Ms. Poule, radiant. A dog growled behind the door. Luke's hand left for a frantic tour of his pockets to find the mace before the door opened and out rushed rover.

He heard the dog being swatted with a rolled up newspaper. Whining. A skinny, stubble-faced, bathrobed figure with a paintbrush in hand and cigarette in his mouth pushed open the screen door to get a better look over the funny-faced caller.

"What?"

"I'm looking for Alica Poule. A good friend, Professor Boil, told me she'd be here."

"Well, buddy," said the painter transferring the paintbrush to his left hand to be able to take the cigarette out of his mouth, "you're about two hours too late. She and me just had a fight."

Luke blinked several times.

"She's gone."

"You know where to, Mr...?"

"Les. Les Stake. Like I said...?"

"Pat Byrd."

"Bird, huh? Well, we had a fight and whoom, she's on her way. Hot temper. Fights about anything. I wouldn't stop what I doing to bring her another cup of coffee into the bathroom where she's reading in the tub."

"What's she read?"

"A lot of shit. Today it was something by Max Planck."

"Who's that?"

"Some scientist. Used to work for Hitler, I think."

"Know where she was...?"

"Not with me to Hawaii, she said. I just landed a one year teaching job out at their be-easy-on-me university."

"Friend of mine's out there now," Wentworth said while simultaneously being hit by the intuition that Edward was in paradise no more—that he was scraped into a plastic bag down at the morgue.

"Hey! You feel sick?"

"Kind of."

"Well, come in a minute."

"I'm allergic to dogs. Thanks, anyway. I'll be all right. Any idea of where she might have gone?"

"Several. You want to hear 'em all?"

"Please."

It was too bad. Maybe he was good, but the painter definitely showed signs of a developing arthritis in his hands.

"Who did you say you were chasing her for, pal?"

Luke was staring irritating at Les' hands. Went looked abashedly up, apology written across the cover of his shameful mug. Answer, please.

"I'm a claims investigator for the Unlimited Insurance Agency. Professor Boil is alleging Ms. Poule broke an object de art, a Chinese funeral horse from the sixth century. We have to confirm that it wasn't done maliciously."

"You mean that fartful old turd has money to buy Chinese horses, but is too cheap and dumb to buy anything from me?"

"Actually it's more complicated because apparently the statue was originally a gift from Ms. Poule to Professor Boil." Wentworth removed his sunglasses and rubbed his sweaty brow before re-stationing his shields. "And it's a case of whose property she destroyed. Hers or his."

"She's been buying that microscopic scopophiliac presents?!"

"Can I please learn where Ms. Poule is now?"

"Insurance investigator eh?" Stake said looking Wentworth up and down. "A," said Stake, putting his brush in his pocket and counting away on his fingers, "she's gone back to her poppa, which I doubt, so make that minus A. She's lately screwed up one of his deals for him. A, she's lighted around John Wicked-Wang Carter's pole. He's a wine grower up in the valley, makes the stuff the French are all worried about. B, (second finger pushed firmly down) she's at speed Rick's. He runs a car nut's heaven on the strip. Rick, the stick, Moynihan."

"How do you write that person's last name?"

Stake spelled it out.

Then came "C." C was a drug dealer who supplied the great white way for Alica and all others who could afford it. That man was bad and hard. Alica wouldn't stay there for long. Why bother trying to cut through the guy's muscle, right?

"D," was that Alica was at Momma Susan's. Boil was not the only peep freak in town. Alica loved to snoop when she was low or after getting high. Address provided. Mansionville again.

"E." If she wasn't off her "science-got-the-mojo" trip yet, she'd head over to John Capon's apartment. A bright boy from the laser lab at U.C.L.A. on Cambridge Street near Harvard. Fortunately, that was it. Four easy leads. A regular case. Luke expressed his gratitude and stupidly squeezed Stake's hand when saying goodbye.

The dog barked from inside the house as Wentworth climbed into his car. He could hear sudden yelping as if someone had accidentally stepped on its tail. Luke was hungry and stopped at the first place he could find. It turned out it was a health food haven. He was craving cuttlefish, sturgeon and fried octopus. He got a bean salad and some yogurt.

A phone call revealed a drive to Napa Valley was unnecessary. Carter was on a diplomatic mission to the Ruhr for a week, had left three days ago. Another phone call disclosed that Moynihan was in traction at the hospital with a spike in his head to heal a broken neck.

"Car accident?"

"No, failure to pay gambling debts," the wise-ass employee said. It was no big secret. Rick was your typical "too rich for brains" bully and nobody cared what bad things befell him.

The Brentwood cathouse became Luke's destiny. You put it on your credit card these days, you know.

Momma Susan sounds like a fat woman's name. Someone

who dresses in low-cut dresses and has boobs bobbing out that show a map full of veins. Susan was in her early thirties, tall and trim without gaudy make-up who wore New York fashions. Luke was the gross article as far in what was a tastefully decorated hotel-type operation.

"Take off those sunglasses before you begin talking to me. You look like a pixilated piece of plasma with those on. What's your name?" Ms. Susan commanded the lax lump that sat across from her.

"Les Bowman." Wentworth removed the glasses and revealed a surprising pair of intelligent eyes. They flustered the lady slightly, made her aware a game was being played. She trimmed her attitude commensurately. "I'm looking for Ms. Poule. I was told she sometimes comes in."

"What's your business? We don't go around telling stories about our customers. I wouldn't be in…."

"I've been hired by her father to help clear her of a charge of complicity in a murder case."

"So, who's dead?" The lady smugly lighted up, arching her back in her chair, arms pushing against the top of the desk like a cat stretching its paws on a carpet.

"Luke Wentworth."

"The detective who was blown up in his kitchen? That was reported as a leaky gas line."

"How could it be when the fellow had an electric stove?"

"What?"

"Look," said Bowman conjuring a stare of utmost sincerity to shoot the now attentive businesswoman, "if I don't find her before the people she's crossed do, you'll be light a client."

The madame was reflecting. The clothes he was wearing must be a disguise. No one as sharp as this could have such repellent taste. "Follow me." She pressed a button under the desk and a door swung open to the left. "We can keep secrets, can't we?"

"I throw away the keys to treasure houses every day because I know I have to."

The madame was telling herself to be sure and have Mr. Bowman leave his card.

He was led down a dark corridor by Momma's familiar hand. About twenty-five paces on, the madame removed a disc (magnetic—the hall was soundproof. You could even turn on the lights if you wanted to, but that killed people's love of the Gothic. The apertures were coated with a screen that didn't leak away secrets) and invited Louie to take a look.

Dinner was being served. Two people were seated at a table attended by a frisky waiter. The female was out of range to the right. Wentworth could see a stout oriental businessman with a huge watch on his wrist. He performed tricks on the watch calculator between bites of his mountain trout. Occasionally, a hand would reach across the table to check and confirm the computation.

"Want to hear what they're saying?"

The voice made Luke jump.

"It's all right, honey. Everything's soundproof. The old days, having to hold your breath while you watch, are gone."

"When are they going to get rid of the table so I can see that angel's bottom?"

"Never, silly. Can't you tell Mr. Mitsu is a homosexual, teasing himself with the waiter while a young and ravishing girl has to look on, disappointed and rejected?"

"They look more like they're discussing a deal."

"And so they are, bright boy. Simultaneous events are very in this year...." Sue flipped a switch that confirmed wave and particle, undyingly together. The man was talking steel, plexiglass, shipbuilding, oyster beds and beer. This woman did not purr contentment in return, but asked about precise dates, prices, plans.

So! Alica was very much a part of the expanding Poule universe. No wonder daddy was so upset about her departure. "Want to see her?"

"Sure. How?"

"I just change the lens, my boy. Not much to see yet."

"Does the executive know that what he's saying is being recorded?"

"No need. She remembers everything." Sue screwed the fish-eye lens place and invited Bowman's eye to it.

"Goddamnit!"

"What's the matter?"

"That's Judith Poule!" said L.B.L.W. through gritted teeth.

"Why, of course."

"I want Alica!!!"

"Hey, quiet. We're not that soundproof."

Curse mated with curse as Wentworth stalked back down the hall beating a fist on the wall. Sue chased after trying to stop the ruination of her business by this man turned monster. Wentworth could hear her coming, so he increased his pace. He was moving out of the driveway before she came through the front door damning his name. "Bowman, your ass won't be worth shark bait when I catch up to you!"

Luke headed for John Capon's apartment. Checking his rear view mirror, he could see Judith Poule's silver Jaguar doing 100 mph. Crazy, dodging traffic, after his butt.

She was, indirectly, after all, his employer. He put his foot to the floor and tried to outrun her for a few blocks. Red light! He reached over and locked the passenger side door as she screeched up.

She pulled a gun out of her purse as she got out and seemed

upset. Wentworth ran the light. She must know by now that it was him. Why was she so riled?

Luke pulled into the parking lot of a restaurant and rushed inside. "Table for two," he told the maître d'. Ms. Poule found him about to be seated with her, to dinner. "Cocktails?" Judith commanded a martini be brought. Luke timidly tried to request a cola, but she changed his order to a Double Bloody Mary.

They squared off. "What's little Luke doing spying through peepholes?"

"I thought you were going to be your sister."

"I was told that—Oh, thank you." The drinks arrived. A menu was placed in the male's hands and he couldn't resist a review. Judith tore it from him. Wentworth had to explain the details to Judith without ever hearing a word about what she was in such a stew about. "Drink your drink," was about all she had to say. After about three quarters of an hour, she was satisfied that Luke didn't know how to use what he had heard and let it drop. Judith apologized for losing control and told Wentworth to report to her about Alica as soon as he found her. She was for Wentworth going to see the drug dealer. Wentworth pointed out that he looked two shades on the narc side.

Should he be going around to a fortress like that? She insisted. Wentworth flushed Ms. Poule's advice away as soon as she exited. He went to the bar to chase away the foul taste of tomato tenaciously lining his throat.

XXXIV. IN WHICH WE WRENCH TO A CONCLUSION AND WENTWORTH WAKES UP

It would definitely be an asset if we could make ourselves aware of how much of what we do is just an expression of the behavioral boundaries that are extensions of our genetically implanted potentials. For the few of us who are brainless, it doesn't much matter if the world works in favor the Great Glyph. Otherwise, when we're looking over our shoulder at who's coming and what's past, the ache and misery of being assailable asserts itself. Reason tells us that it will be awhile before a shrimp learns how to whistle. The choice of who butchers you isn't enough, is it? Look around you, Luke. Who are your friends?

Luke's eyes were moving all around as he ascended the steps of the Axis Apartments. He was also chewing his nails. Boil might be found by now. A whole day of classes missed, students with questions, excuses to make about papers not going to be turned in. Wasn't it near midterm?

On the first landing, Luke was bumped into by a scraggly

woman in a quilted housecoat. She grabbed onto Wentworth demanding to know whether or not he had seen her bird.

"Please help me find Bobby," she pleaded. "He's bright blue and talks."

"What kind of bird is it?"

"A parakeet," she cooed.

"Well, how long since you lost your bird?"

"Only about an hour. Oh, please. Won't you help me look for him?"

"Sure. Right after I come back down. I've got to go up to get something from a friend who's on his way out."

"You won't help me! You've got the face of a liar!"

Luke saw that he had to get away from this mess before it surrounded him. He pushed his way past.

"A liar!" she screeched into his ear. "A liar!" he heard as he hurried up the stairs, sorry he couldn't find the bird and crush it in his palm.

When Boil had recovered, some hours ago, he was able to tell Dranthus his tale. Boil wanted someone to go right out and capture Luke alive. Aloysius had plans for the boy. Dranthus reminded Boil that Wentworth's appearance, mode of transportation, and next destination were all unknown to them. Besides, such decisions were out of their hands. Boil sat up in the bed and crossed his arms. "What I say gets done!"

Dranthus burst out laughing at Buddah Boil. But he was too close to Boil's to be doing that. Boil bounced Edgar in the stomach and had his own laugh in return. The stooge show of power would have continued had not the doctor come in to tell Dranthus that there was a call for him in the office. Aloysius was rocketed to paranoialand and shouted, "Why isn't it me that the call's for?"

"Relax, only a girlfriend trying to get Edgar to pay some

attention," the doctor told Boil.

Aloysius glared at the both of them. "You're a farting little swine's prick, Tropp. You two are conspiring to usurp my directorship."

And so they were, and so they were. Boil tried to get out of bed. The doctor encouraged him to get back in—between shouts for a male nurse who proved too big for Boil.

Tropp had his guard stand by the bed as he blew tiny notes of comfort and reassurance into Boil's jealous ears. *They'd* never talked to Dranthus seriously before. He was a hothead always wanting to move too fast. If people didn't sit on Edgar Albert Dranthus, disasters were sure. Why, once he'd even proposed … But that's off the subject. Boil turned his hatred inward and masochistically owned up to the fact that Alica Poulc might not be all that in love with him. Abandoning her daddy's empire to throw in with his crowd of new world planners wasn't a step made out of worship to his "new world" vision. Thought.

Right reason had prevailed in Dranthus about the hustling honey from the moment she had spurned his advance. Alica had continued to play Joan of Arc for the benefit of "Pops" Boil.

On the phone, Dranthus explained the circumstances as objectively as possible to the military arm. Identity of Wentworth ascertained. Chop the link.

Nate had had a good time up in the North Woods. He'd taken along *In Our Time* and snickered at it by Coleman lantern after doing yoga exercises. He snickered at most everything. If it could have, the flesh would have fallen off of him, ashamed of being stretched over such a nihilistic core. Nate was especially proficient at recognizing patterns. Luke also had a skill for it, but not devotion. They both enjoyed interrupting them.

Stake's was also Nate's starting place and he asked the same questions as Wentworth. Nate was only two and a half hours behind. Stake told Nate about the insurance man who had been by. Any connection? Stake was suspicious, but Natee's phony FBI identification was able to make a strong case that he was the rightful party.

Nate was more aware and informed about Ms. Poule's habits than Wentworth. Naturally, Mr. Poule, in wanting to protect his daughter's reputation, had not told all there was to tell about his precious to his hireling. It was more a question in Nate's mind as to where she would go after she scored, rather than from whom she scored.

After making the same number of phone calls and receiving the same quantums of information, Nate went directly to John Capon's apartment. He dismissed the cat house as a possibility because Alica liked to be around friends, in a relaxing, "no ugly faces" atmosphere when she "went away."

Luke knocked on the door, but no one answered. He noticed that it was open a crack and let himself in. He could hear soft, groaning music. Turning the corner to the left into the first room, there was the laser beam expert, a bullet cranked into his heart, sprawled back in a coffee stained old easy chair.

Luke cursed. They'd been there and gotten the girl. He had no leads and he'd have to start all over again. He walked up to the corpse and shut its eyes. A dumbfounded expression remained on the face—a look that said, "Hey, how'd you get in the front door. Am I so screwed up that I forgot to lock it? Uh-ohh. You look like a narc! What's that gun for?" *FFFttt.* One shot. No convulsing. The girl who's in the other room probably doesn't even hear it.

Wentworth shut off the radio and held his head. Pain swarmed through it. He looked at Capon, reached over and twisted his stiff features into a kind of contented smile.

"That's how death should look," he told the corpse. "Times

are getting more anxious. Have you noticed that?" "Yeah, I have too. How's your research going?" At this point, Wentworth's imagination had Capon alive and answering the sort of questions John probably got asked every day by people who didn't know a maser from a phaser or a laser. And, like all people who want to learn just a little and not a drop more from any minor deity they've been asking questions of—if you ask and find out too much, self-questioning begins, and that leads to self-abnegation and that to discontentment with one's entire scope and focus upon life—Luke stopped the exchange, which was beginning to escape the layman anyway. They shifted around in the listener's cranial deposit boxes for later sorting, for forgetfulness. Now Luke, patting Capon on the head excused himself and began his search for aspirin.

Finding the bathroom, he strode up to the medicine cabinet and, opening the mirrored door, he browsed. Capon had quite a selection of prescription drugs. Luke wondered if they helped him think, actually stimulated his research, or dulled and opiated him along with the rest of humanity they served.

Luke took six aspirins, ran the water, and scooped it to his mouth with cupped hands. He closed the cabinet door and surveyed his face. The eyes had acquired bags. Were they going on a trip? They certainly needed rest.

Luke picked up Capon's razor and carefully trimmed his moustache. Staring intently over his shoulder, he could see a red line through the shower glass doors behind him. What was that? It could be cloth couldn't it? Jock strap? Red? Who knows what Capon was into. The shower glass was gouged and faceted so it was impossible to make anything out. Wentworth tried to concentrate on what new moves his face could make. The computer wouldn't let him stay dead for too long. His fingerprints were safely on file around the murdered man's apartment. Luke was only in the mud up to his waist, so he wasn't going to squawk about a few more inches. He was leaving a trail to assemble some insurance.

That red line bothered him again. Wentworth turned and opened the shower door. Nate had slit her throat while she was shot up to the gills. She was still in the lotus position she had assumed.

Luke dropped to his knees and hunched over the toilet bowl. The dry heaves. Half an hour after that, he wandered around the apartment, found a bottle, came back to the bathroom, pulled down the seat, pulled shots and cried a while either staring directly at the girl's face or craning his head towards the ceiling or comfortless walls.

There were no more chances. Luke tried to look himself in the mirror. He was a gasping, sobbing, hysterically shivering mask out of control. Stripped of defense and confidence. He was obviously a target too, although he didn't know much. Whoever caught him wouldn't let him go. The police, the FBI; whoever they were—even in custody he wouldn't be safe. Did he want to live anymore? No more Luke Wentworth whatsoever? It came down to that now. He didn't even look like his passport photo.

Packard's last gift to Wentworth: keep enough money, $5000 at minimum, stashed along with your passport. In this business, you're bound to fall into things, into situations in which the circumstances dictate that you disappear for awhile.

He'd have to go South, into Mexico. There he could reassume his identity, then change it. This wouldn't be a short exile. He would have to watch the papers, keep up on what was moving.

Wentworth looked into the mirror, back at the girl. Should he kill Boil for her? Walk up to Boil in another disguise and…? But just look at the time! The cops would be on their way. It was already called in.

Central or South America, where you don't need an occupation or definite skills. Where your money will go a ways, where you can invest, afford land. Otherwise, there's no hope of living except above the poverty line. Germany, Japan and France aren't buying used detectives. New York City seems so hard to work. L.A., the only place in the world for the kind of operation you've been running.

Alica animated herself for the drunken, sobbing, grieving clown and began to berate him. "Why weren't you here sooner? Why are you still such a self-fancying, weak-willed slob?" Ms. Poule jerked herself up, stepped out of the shower and put a white hand on the going-insane detective's shoulders.

"You know, I've had thoughts about you. Wondered what you're like. Waited as long as I could."

In the blink of an eye, Alica was back in her cold water, staring limpidly at the tile. Luke couldn't take too much more now. A look down at the floor and a look up. She was standing, beckoning Luke to approach, curling a finger of the hand.

Running out of the front door, Luke stepped on the dizzy woman's lost parakeet as it strolled, booble-footedly along the length of the landing.

The End.

Please visit

PageBacon.com

for more exciting titles